### "The unifo[rm] [has got to go,]" Tyler said.

"You look like the proverbial French maid in a bad movie," he added.

"I *what*?" Cheyenne exclaimed.

"You are an exotically beautiful woman, and I find the uniform distracting, as adolescent as that sounds. You must know the effect you have on a man who appreciates natural beauty in all its forms."

"Well, I never would have believed anybody could deliver that line with a straight face."

"If you can't handle honesty—"

"Oh, I can handle it, but just what would you like me to wear in place of this alluring domestic uniform?"

"Suit yourself," he answered lightly. Then he abruptly stepped forward, and she felt his thumb and forefinger curl under her chin. "Just remember. I am an intense man—emotional, passionate—and it has been two long and lonely years since I enjoyed the full companionship of a woman."

Her eyes widened. Two years? She had her doubts. Still . . . no one could say she hadn't been warned. . . .

Dear Reader:

Happy holidays! All the best wishes to you for a joyful, loving holiday season with your family and friends.

And while celebrating, I hope that you think of Silhouette Romance. Our authors join me in wishing you a wonderful holiday season, and we have some treats in store for you during November and December—as well as during the exciting new year.

Experience the magic that makes the world so special for two people falling in love. Meet heroines who will make you cheer for their happiness and heroes (be they the boy next door or a handsome, mysterious stranger) who will win your heart. Silhouette Romances reflect the magic of love—sweeping you away with books that will make you laugh and cry, heartwarming, poignant stories that will move you time and time again.

During the next months, we're publishing romances by many of your all-time favorites such as Diana Palmer, Brittany Young, Lucy Gordon and Victoria Glenn. Your response to these authors and others in Silhouette Romances has served as a touchstone for us, and we're pleased to bring you more books with Silhouette's distinctive medley of charm, wit and—above all—*romance*.

I hope you enjoy this book and the many stories to come. Come home to Silhouette romance—for always!

Sincerely,

Tara Hughes
Senior Editor
Silhouette Books

# ARLENE JAMES

# The Discerning Heart

Published by Silhouette Books New York

**America's Publisher of Contemporary Romance**

SILHOUETTE BOOKS
300 E. 42nd St., New York, N.Y. 10017

ISBN: 0-373-08614-8

First Silhouette Books printing November 1988

Printed in the U.S.A.

## *ARLENE JAMES*

grew up in Oklahoma and has lived all over the South. In 1976 she married "the most romantic man in the world," and since then "every trip with him has been a romance to remember forever." We think you will feel the same way about her books.

# Chapter One

Cheyenne Cates stood before the black lacquered door trimmed with rods of gleaming brass and a handle of thick, leaded crystal etched in patterns of diamonds and leaves. She felt suddenly as if she'd stepped off the sidewalk onto the broad, brick-faced stoop and into a foreign world. This was not the Santa Fe she was accustomed to—the town that fitted about her with the same comfort and ease as her soft, old leather vest.

Right now Cheyenne was wearing the vest layered over a faded chambray blouse and a white eyelet camisole tied with delicate ribbons of palest pink—the same pink as that of the double petticoat that peeked from below the heavily embroidered hem of her full brown skirt. She had thought the skirt and the heavy, hand-tooled concho belt the most beautiful articles of attire she'd ever seen when she'd bought them from the old Indian woman's booth at the spring festival, but standing now before this large, slick door, she felt frowsy and out of place.

She wished she'd had her hair cut. Every few months for years now, even since before they'd dropped out of college together, her friend Vicky had trimmed the ends of her hair where the wild, billowing, red-orange locks faded to a pale, muddy color that she hated. At times since Vicky had gotten her hairdresser's license, she had tried to convince Cheyenne to cut it in some short, fashionable style that would be both sophisticated and easy to manage. But Cheyenne couldn't imagine herself without the long, wild tresses swishing below her shoulder blades. Wet and straight, her hair hung almost to her waist, but when dry the natural curl ate up the length and left it bunched thick and springy in the middle of her back. About her face it scrunched in deep, hardy waves and twisted into odd ringlets that moved with each of her sure, direct steps.

At the moment, however, she felt neither sure nor direct. She felt . . . inferior. And, oh, how she despised that. Marilyn had always made her feel that way, and just knowing Marilyn was behind that lacquered door with its imposing brass fittings and elegant handle made her feel small and useless and angry. She couldn't think for the moment why she'd even agreed to come here. Perhaps it was the shock of hearing her old classmate's voice over the phone or the prestigious name of the Bray Gallery—or the fact that she was once more without a job and the prospect of displaying her work in so influential a gallery as the Bray, was too much to pass up. That in mind, she clutched the trio of small canvases in the sling beneath her arm and steeled herself for what lay beyond.

The door swung open easily when Cheyenne pulled, and a sigh of cool air reached out to her in chilly invitation. It was summer, the last week of July, and the Santa Fe air was heavy with sunshine. She liked the heat, really, yet the artificial cool was always a relief. It made her think of the snow and ski slopes high up on the mountain and their cold, dazzling white light.

She walked through the door, the stacked wooden heels of her cowboy boots muffled by deep, wine-red carpet. The place was not just quiet but silent, with fat, smooth white marble columns filling and defining the room, each hung with a painting in a gilt frame. All the paintings were smallish and dark and traditional. With a sinking feeling she thought of the vibrant colors and strong lines of the paintings beneath her arm. They were good, she knew, but how good? Good enough for the Bray Gallery? The feeling of displacement grew as she strolled into the main gallery between two enormous columns holding up ornate brass and crystal sconces flickering with electric lights. The place was a virtual forest of columns bearing sweet, gentle little paintings, but between them she glimpsed spaces of strikingly colored walls where larger, more progressive works were displayed. Taking heart, she journeyed farther into the forest. Almost immediately a somber, imposing figure stepped into her path.

"May I help you?" His tone was nasal and slightly condescending, exactly what one would expect from this tall, gaunt male with his large, thin nose and black, funereal suit. He sniffed at her and raised a pale, graceful hand to indicate the canvases. "We don't look at unsolicited work." He tried to make it sound kind and failed. Cheyenne smirked at him.

"Well, we're in luck, Bella. Mrs. Bray sent for me."

"Bella?" he inquired solicitously, his attitude changing abruptly at the name of his employer.

"As in Lugosi," she quipped dryly. "And my name's Cates, Cheyenne Cates."

"How droll," he responded, looking exactly like the stereotypical undertaker, hands folded, brows drawn together over narrow, deep-set eyes. "I'll announce you." He made a military turn and strode away. "Oh, Madam," he said, "there's a quaint young lady here by the name of Cates." Cheyenne had to smile. Animosity she could deal with.

Several minutes passed before Marilyn appeared, and at first sight of her old college mate Cheyenne felt out of her depth again. Marilyn hadn't changed a whit, except that her black hair seemed a little blacker and was swept onto the side and top of her head in a pair of large, sleek waves, ending in a long, blunt ponytail behind her right ear. Cheyenne took in the black-on-cream polka-dotted peplum jacket over the short, black skirt, the stiletto heels and a pair of teardrop pearls before Marilyn engulfed her in a cloud of overpowering scent and a very uncharacteristic hug. On second look the jacket and skirt were silk, and the pearls dangled from studs set with diamonds.

"Darling!" Marilyn gushed. "Ignore old Stephen. He's wonderful help but rather imposing and a bit protective. But one doesn't want to complain, does one?"

For the second time Cheyenne found herself smiling. "No, one doesn't," she managed to say, then cleared her throat and tried for a certain decorum. "He was quite—proper—actually."

"Yes, of course, he would be. But, oh, darling, it's so good to see you again, and you're looking so...so...like yourself." Marilyn fluttered her red nails, trying to gloss over the small faux pas. Cheyenne was not amused this time, perhaps because she felt so frumpy and out of place and too much like a down-on-her-luck friend—acquaintance, really—seeking a handout. Still, Marilyn had called her.

"Okay, Stucky," she said, purposely using an old nickname. Stucky Stiles, most stuck-up coed on campus, only it was Stucky Bray now, young widow of one of the art colony's most enduring and elderly patrons. Best to remember that. "I was glad to hear from you," she went on in a kinder tone. "Surprised but glad. Now what's it all about?"

Marilyn fluttered her fingers again. "Oh. Your canvases!" she exclaimed. "Come in the office, and we'll take a look at them." She was all smiles and grand gestures, but Cheyenne had the feeling she was covering up an uncharacteristic nervousness. She followed Marilyn's swaying hips through the maze of cool columns to a door covered with red leather and studded with brass tacks. Behind it was a short, narrow hallway almost blocked by an ornate marble water fountain flanked by fat, cherubic Cupids. At the end of the hallway another leather-covered door opened into a spacious sitting room filled to overflowing with velvet couches and petite wing chairs. The faint smell of tobacco hung in the air, and Cheyenne guessed that Marilyn had never broken her college smoking habit.

Beyond the sitting room was the office. This room, too, was large and, taken with the sitting room, totally incongruous with the remainder of the gallery. Cheyenne was flatly taken aback by the sight of a bare black wall with red, flocked, wave-patterned wallpaper on the wainscot, the red fading on adjacent walls to scarlet then pink, from flamingo to the palest, baby-girl hue and back to red again in the center of the opposite wall. The black was shock enough, but the ceiling-to-floor waves of red undulating through the pinks was ghastly, especially when taken with the ornate ebony desk detailed in gold and the velvet furnishings. There was one particularly appalling lamp designed to look like a bird cage on a crook stand. Cheyenne stared slack jawed.

"Yes," Marilyn said, her pride obvious, "it is stunning, isn't it?" Cheyenne could only nod, her mouth flapping shut with a snap. "My Wilson, God rest his soul, was a great

judge and lover of art, a generous, trusting man, but he
was—how shall I say it?—conservative.'' She laughed. It
had a practiced air about it. "Stuffy, even. His age, I suppose—which is not to say he wasn't an exciting, virile man.''
That, too, sounded practiced, but what came next was like
a vignette from a bad play. She sniffed and lifted her
professionally manicured fingers to dab at the corners of her
eyes. Her hands trembled, as did the little sigh that she allowed to escape her pursed lips. Cheyenne had to bat her
eyes to keep from rolling them. Then, abruptly, the scene
ended. "Now," Marilyn said, striding to the blank, black
wall. "Let's see what you've brought me."

Cheyenne set her canvases at her feet, then lifted them one
at a time into Marilyn's waiting hands, so that Marilyn
could hang them on a series of black-painted nails. After
spending some time arranging them, Marilyn studied each
critically. Once she even got out a little magnifying glass and
studied a blue section of what Cheyenne felt was a truly
unique rendering of a nineteenth-century vamp and her
modern counterpart, one stiff and strangely proper in her
corset and plumed hat, the other in miniskirt and T-shirt,
complete with punk hairdo.

The work was from a series Cheyenne was doing that
contrasted women from two centuries in comparable roles.
Of the other two paintings in the trio that she had brought,
one dealt with women as prospective mothers, both preg-
nant—one exultantly so, the other in great fear. The other
work portrayed women as students, one figure poring over
her studies with dogged desperation, the other gabbing on
the phone, her books haphazardly strewn across her desk.
Cheyenne had in each instance painted her dual subjects in
a single setting, subtly emphasizing their differences.

At length Marilyn moved to the corner of her desk and sat
down. "Well," she said, "I think we can use these. Not right

away, of course. We've a full house at the moment, but in a few weeks or months . . ." She let her sentence trail away.

Cheyenne felt a bitter sense of disappointment. So much for making this month's rent. The manager would give her a few more days, she was sure, but she hated with a passion to impose, and it couldn't go on forever. Her feelings must have shown in her face. Marilyn clucked her tongue. "Now, now, darling. I know you're in a tight spot. I heard you'd, ah, left your employment."

Cheyenne smirked. "You heard I belted Leo Gilbert in full view of a party of twelve at a formal dinner hosted by his wife for the Committee for Preservation of the Arts in Historical Santa Fe."

Marilyn demurred and scratched—elegantly, of course— behind one ear. "And, um, did you?"

"Right in the kisser." She rocked one fist. "Pow."

Marilyn stifled a laugh. "Cheyenne! You're as wild as your name, I swear. What on earth possessed you to do such a thing?"

"Well, I warned him," she said with a shrug. "I told him the next time he patted, pinched or played with something that didn't belong to him, I was going to let him have it, no matter where, no matter what. I guess he thought he'd be safe in front of the Committee for the Preservation of the Arts in Historical Santa Fe, but I'd said no matter where— and I meant it."

"But you're the one without the job now," Marilyn pointed out.

Cheyenne turned away, not wanting Marilyn to see the desperation she felt. "Gives me more time to paint," she said offhandedly. "You really think you might show these?"

"I think we might even be able to do a private showing," came the too-quick reply.

Cheyenne turned around, surprised. "You're kidding."

"We'd need many more paintings, of course. You mentioned a series. I suppose there are others like these."

"In various stages."

"Well, when you finish them, we'll take another look. Until then, maybe I can help you in another way. Maybe we can help each other."

Still stunned by the prospect of a private showing, Cheyenne looked at her old dorm mate. It would mean a one-woman show, a debut, and in one of the best houses in the country. It was mind-boggling, yet at the same time it felt inevitable. She had always known on some level that one day she would have her moment in the sun. She was an artist, a painter, and soon the world would know that, too. People, strangers would see and want and appreciate her work. Not that she hadn't sold paintings—quite a few, in fact—in malls and fairs and festivals. But a private showing! *From private maid to private showing,* she thought. *It's about time.* Almost.

"I might as well be honest with you," Marilyn was saying. "I have my reasons for calling you, and they have less to do with your art—though I am pleased to note your progress—than with my concerns for someone else."

"I—I don't get it."

Marilyn smiled thinly and walked around her desk. "You remember my sister, Leah?"

"Yes, of course. Leah was the..." She'd almost said "nice one" but managed to amend it to "oldest." Marilyn seemed not to notice. She lowered herself most regally into her chair.

"Well, my darling Leah is gone, dead." She sniffed again and waved a red-tipped hand. "Everyone who truly cared for me is gone," she went on bitterly, and this time the grief seemed genuine. "My parents, grandparents, Wilson and Leah." Cheyenne felt a surge of pity for her, remembering how no one had liked Marilyn in college, how the popular, older Leah had towed her along in her wake of laughter and goodwill, kept her in the limelight, won acceptance for her despite Marilyn's snobbery and obvious disdain for her fellow students. Cheyenne had liked Leah, though they had not been intimate friends, and had tolerated Marilyn because of it. Leah had been so popular she'd seemed almost unapproachable; yet she had been genuinely likable, and Cheyenne was truly saddened to think of her death. She could not help wondering how Marilyn, who was not likable, survived without her personal mentor.

"I didn't know. How did it happen?" she asked softly.

"She fell. That vile husband of hers forced her up on the mountain and she fell, skiing. They said it was an accident, but no one will ever convince me of that. You know how athletic she was, how graceful and healthy. And him with that nasty temper, that impatience. He was jealous, I tell you. Men naturally appreciate a stunningly beautiful woman." Her tone implied experience in the area. "He couldn't stand it when men looked at her!"

"Was there an inquiry?"

"No." She seemed less certain now, less forceful. "Do you honestly think anyone in this town would question the veracity of Tyler Crawford?"

Cheyenne's mouth dropped open. "*The* Tyler Crawford?"

"Who else? And there, doesn't that prove my point? Look at you. Just mention the name and people fall all over themselves."

"Marilyn, the man's a national institution!"

"And an ogre!"

She didn't know what to say, what to believe. Tyler Crawford was renowned as one of the definitive talents of the time. True, the man was reclusive to the point of paranoia by some accounts and remained removed from the very cultural organization that had championed him so tirelessly. And yet... *Fragile Tragedy in Snow,* depicted the lifeless, bleeding form of an eagle crumpled against a landscape of icy white. Far from being gruesome, the painting was instead poignant, making one think of the tragedy of solitary death, the crime of such death, the endangerment of the species, the mindless inhumanity of man—even the fragile strength and surprising vulnerability of the nation claiming the bird as its symbolic soul. The sensitivity of the work had left her breathless, as thinking of it did now.

"Marilyn," she said finally, "I don't understand what I have to do with any of this."

The other woman wrung her hands, and Cheyenne recognized in the gesture the craving for a cigarette. "It's my nephew," she said. "Leah's son, my only family. Oh, Cheyenne, I'm worried sick about him." She did seem distraught, so much so that Cheyenne herself felt disturbed.

"Are you saying Tyler Crawford mistreats his son?"

"I'm saying I don't know! How can I when the fiend won't even allow me near the boy? Oh, Cheyenne, I was at my wit's end. And then...then I heard about the incident with Leo, and, well, the description fit you to a tee, so I did some asking around—discreetly, of course—and I found that it *was* you, still playing the part of the maid. I remembered, you see, that you used to do that sort of thing in college. We thought it quaint at the time...."

"Those of you wealthy enough to employ maids of your own."

"Oh, darling, don't be mean to me. You don't know how elated I was to discover you again after all this time. You're my salvation, my only hope, and the beauty of it is that I'll be helping you while you're helping me!"

"Never mind how you're going to help me. Just how am I going to help you?" Cheyenne asked suspiciously. She had a horrible feeling she knew the answer, and the first bitter twinges of disappointment were already assailing her.

"I'm going to help you," Marilyn told her deliberately, "by telling you of a position now available for a housemaid in the home of Tyler Royce Crawford, and by supplying you with references necessary to secure that position."

Cheyenne let that sink in. Tyler Crawford was looking for a maid. She was a maid. Tyler Crawford was one of the greatest living painters in the world. She was a painter. What she might learn just by being around him was enough to give her gooseflesh. Add to that the fact that she had no legitimate references from her last job to aid her in acquiring another and the prospect was enticing all on its own. But there were other considerations.

"I repeat," she said, "how am I supposed to help you?"

"By keeping a protective eye on my only living relative, my nephew. It's my hope, eventually, to document Tyler's abuse of him and possibly gain custody—if my suspicions are true, that is."

It sounded legitimate, reasonable, even commendable. Still . . .

"And what about my showing?" Cheyenne asked.

Marilyn stood and strode around the desk, her gaze on the paintings. "You understand, Cheyenne, if you do this favor for me, it does not mean I can guarantee you a showing. The reputation of this gallery is far too important to be compromised by inferior work. This, however, is quite remarkable. If the other canvases, say six or seven more, are as good as these, I think we can put together a mutually profitable program."

Cheyenne was satisfied, her suspicions mollified. "Good," she said. "But about the references . . ."

Marilyn lifted an imperious hand. "Never fear. I might employ a little chicanery, but I'll not stoop to outright deceit. The reference will come from Leo Gilbert himself. It is, after all, deserved, is it not? Just leave the matter to me."

That was a real bit of satisfaction to Cheyenne. This just might be her lucky day, after all. And who would have thought the source would be old Stucky Stiles herself? Cheyenne shook her head, and Marilyn's dark, stylized brows drew together in a crease. To ease her doubt Cheyenne laughed and put out her hand. As Marilyn's cool, smooth palm met hers, she sealed it.

"Marilyn, darling," she said with a touch of mimicry, "you've got your cagey self a deal." They were both laughing when supercilious Stephen called "Madam Bray" back to her business.

The house was enormous. It hung over the city, commanding the mountainside and dwarfing the piñon pines that surrounded it. Moblike, the slender trees whispered rumors spread by a languorous wind, while the great glass and lumber and rock house jutted about from one angle and another, sinking broad decks into the mountainside here and retaining walls there, thrusting its peaked tin roofs toward the sun. She thought at first that it was nothing more than a funny old barn, but as she turned this way and that along the narrow road winding its way upward toward it, she changed her opinion. It was a temple, the fresh, eastern sun bouncing gold and silver off the shiny roof and whitening the massive windows.

She followed the road all the way up in her wrinkled and battered old Dodge, bypassing the cutoff that led around to the front of the house on the west and continuing on to the cavernous garage crafted right out of the body of the mountain. One of the four double doors was up, as Mrs.

Mellon had said it would be, but Cheyenne parked her car outside anyway, feeling terribly like a trespasser, and walked inside to find the door with the black buzzer.

As she passed a compact black pickup with dark tinted windows, she paused to assess her appearance one last time, but the distortion of the image made any realistic judgment impossible, and she was forced to settle for straightening the acid-washed denim miniskirt and matching jacket. She thought of Marilyn's advice to dress to "enhance" her "assets." "Tyler's a monster, darling," she had said, "but he's also a man with incredible appetites. It's all right to entice, but keep your distance. He has this fatal charm, and I needn't tell you what your fate would be if he ever learned of our alliance."

Marilyn's warning in mind, Cheyenne turned up the collar of her white, oversize blouse and told herself for the hundredth time that there was a little boy in there who might very well need her protection. It was all the justification she needed for what she was doing—so why did she feel guilty? Pushing that question away, she marched up to the door and gave the buzzer a solid, insistent push. Almost before she'd removed her finger, the door opened and a plump, gray-haired woman in a navy blue dress with white collar and apron greeted her.

"Miss Cates?"

"Yes."

"How nice of you to come. I've made sticky buns and coffee and there are some wonderful oranges for juice. Won't you join me?"

Cheyenne was a little overwhelmed by the warmth of her welcome. The woman had a comfortable, yeasty smell about her reminiscent of Christmas and grandmothers and warm cocoa by the fire. Cheyenne said something vaguely positive and found herself being swept into a clean, bare hall-way on Mrs. Mellon's solid arm.

"That's storage over there," the older woman said in a proud voice. "I tell you, it's a dream. There are closets for the china and silver and for the crystal and the big pots we use for large dinner parties—we don't do much of that any-more, not since Mrs. Crawford died—but anyway.... There's a whole room full of freezers and shelves for canned goods and bins for staples. And, oh, there's the wine cellar down below and an enormous cedar-lined room for linens. Mr. Crawford let me design the whole thing myself when we were planning the house. Now this is the kitchen, and of course it's my favorite room in the whole house."

It was a large room, bright with yellows and blues and polished steel. Strings of garlic and peppers and fat white onions hung from the ceiling amid copper-bottomed pans and white-speckled blue enamelware. The aroma was heav-enly, fresh coffee mingled with roasted pecans and burned sugar. Cheyenne figured she was going to pick up pound-age just by sniffing. Nevertheless, she settled happily atop a blue stool painted with yellow flowers and let Mrs. Mel-lon spoil her with the airiest of popovers drizzled with cara-mel sauce and pecans.

What followed was unlike any job interview she'd ever had before. Mrs. Mellon chatted about her brothers and her late husband and the two sons who lived "down in the city" and came to visit her two or three times a week.

"Don't know when they're going to marry, those two scamps," she confided over her cup. "The youngest, now, he's got a girl—prettiest little thing—but she's Spanish and her daddy's not convinced marriage with an Anglo would be right for her. They seem determined to wait him out, though, and I'm hoping one day they'll get together. The oldest, that's Decker, he just plays the field. He's a sweet

boy but not very settled, always got an eye out for a good
time. I keep telling them, I'm not getting any younger. I'd
like to have grandchildren before I'm too old to enjoy them.
But then there's Royce. That child's an angel, poor babe.
Love him like my son."

"Royce?" Cheyenne queried innocently, the name setting off bells in her head.

"Mr. Tyler's little son. He's kind of a lonely sort, quiet
and withdrawn. I keep telling Mr. T. the boy should have
playmates his own age, but he doesn't pay me any mind. He
seems to think if he's happy stuck off up here, then the boy
ought to be happy, too. Men. They don't understand things
the same way we women do. Oh, it'll be so nice to have another woman around the place!" She leaned across the
kitchen counter and patted Cheyenne on the hand.

Cheyenne laughed. "Does that mean I'm hired?"

"Well, of course you are. Why not? You're experienced
and sweet and prompt, and you indulge old ladies in their
whims. Why, I've been babbling like a brook all morning
and haven't caught a pained expression yet. I think you'll do
fine." Cheyenne was speechless. Mrs. Mellon laughed and
chucked her beneath the chin. "I like uniforms. Keeps us
from worrying about what to wear day to day. I'll get you
one to take home tonight, and then you can start tomorrow, if that's all right with you."

"All right?" Cheyenne exclaimed. "It's wonderful."

"It's settled then. Now I'll get you that uniform, and we'll
take a little tour of the house. Oh, it's a grand house. You're
going to love it. Mr. Tyler designed it himself, you know,
after the missus passed on. Guess it kept him from going off
his head. He's an intense fellow, as you'll find out, but don't
let him bully you and you'll get along fine." With that, she
vanished into her treasure house, admonishing Cheyenne to
have "just one more. And this time try it with a little of that

sweet cream." Cheyenne sighed, wondering how many extra miles she would have to run to stay fit.

She needn't have worried about it. The lofty exterior of the house hid a multitude of levels and stairs, some sweeping and graceful, some winding and tight, others as steep as the mountain itself. It quickly became obvious why Mrs. Mellon needed help. The stairs in the big, exquisite house were simply too much for her. She apologized profusely for becoming winded and slow, but wouldn't stop even when Cheyenne insisted. Her pride in the place was evident. Somehow she'd kept the acres of wood polished and gleaming, but Cheyenne noticed that the champagne-colored carpets had pilled up in place and badly needed vacuuming.

"I just can't lug that cleaner around," Mrs. Mellon confessed. "And, honey, the windows in this place will give you nightmares. That's why we clean by schedule. Otherwise, you'll get behind and never catch up. Even at that, we have to have a crew in twice a year to give them a good going over. But I don't want to frighten you off. There's just one thing you have to remember, and that's to keep out of Mr. Tyler's loft. That's where he paints, and he'll have both our heads if he catches you messing around in there, not that it couldn't use a good cleaning, mind you. Now anything else you need to know, you just ask me. All right?"

They went through the remainder of her basic duties as they went through the rooms of the house. There were too many to count, and she stopped trying after fifteen, which was the upstairs den, as opposed to the formal living room, the playroom, the game room and the sitting room in the master suite. Then, of course, there was the formal dining room, the family dining room, the breakfast nook and the "supper room" in the master suite, not to mention six bedrooms, maids' quarters—which Mrs. Mellon occupied—

eight bathrooms and a sauna that opened via sliding-glass panels onto the pool. Oddly, the largest room in the house, if it could be called that, was the entry hall, a wide expanse of tiled floor with a ceiling that soared three stories above and was hung with expansive chandeliers of brass and frosted glass. Both the living room and the formal dining area opened off of it, and the staircase from the second floor swept downward in a graceful curve that grew gradually broader to a maximum width of fourteen feet at the bottom.

It was stunning, the lot of it, all wood and glass and rock and expensive Spanish tiles in a variety of hand-painted motifs. The unicolor carpet was thick and plush and hardly appeared to have been trod upon in places, and one of the three fireplaces had never been used. Most amazing of all was the artwork around which the house had clearly been designed, paintings that took her breath away: works by Cézanne and D. H. Lawrence, Georgia O'Keeffe and Agnes Martin, native American R. Lee White and the Wyeths, Red Grooms, Donald Judd, even George Catlin. The range was wide and eclectic. Each piece possessed its own impact and was shown to best advantage. In addition there were myriad pieces of small sculpture and casual displays of unique and rare pottery.

It was a treasure trove of special and beautiful things, a stunning house full of stunning artworks, and just as Mrs. Mellon had predicted, she was in love with it well before the last stair had been ascended and the door with the black buzzer closed at her back. Still, she was filled with trepidation and doubts as she guided her trusty old Dodge back down the mountain. Dozens of questions crowded her mind.

Was Tyler Crawford, creator and collector of such beauty, also capable of the cruelty Marilyn suggested? Marilyn had said he kept her from seeing her nephew, and

Mrs. Mellon had implied that he kept the boy from other children his own age. Why? Was he afraid of what the boy might reveal about his treatment? Or was he maniacally possessive as Marilyn had also suggested? On the other hand, could Mrs. Mellon be so caring and warm and trusting if she were working for a true monster? Could a woman like that close her eyes to the mistreatment of a child? Would she protect her employer in order to protect her own job?

It was only after she'd reached her own modest home, a squat bungalow in a converted motor lodge, that she realized that some of the questions were topics she should have brought up herself—like what her wages and hours of work were to be. And then she realized that her hard-won letter of reference was still tucked away in her handbag, unread, and that she had not so much as laid eyes on her mysterious new boss.

# Chapter Two

As luck would have it, Cheyenne's first day on the job was scheduled as "Floor Day," which meant that every floor in the house had to be vacuumed, swept, mopped and/or waxed, depending upon the surface. By the time she'd lugged the heavy vacuum, a mop, a pail, a broom, a waxing attachment, a brush, carpet cleaner, ammonia, vinegar, wax and a dustpan up to the third level of the house, she was truly and understandably exhausted, and she had a new and deep respect for Mrs. Mellon. Her uniform was rumpled, wet in spots and dusty, and her hair was flying out in all directions, all but a little knot of if having escaped the pins at the back of her head. She had unbuttoned the cuffs above her elbows to allow her more ease as she worked, and she had a run in her stockings, which had split at the knee while she was kneeling in order to clean a ten-step flight of carpeted stairs.

Catching sight of herself in a mirror framed in silver and turquoise, she put down her burdens, allowing them to fall in disarray about her. She was attempting to recapture her wild hair, her mouth full of pins, when a door opened at the end of the hall and a man walked out.

He was not a particularly handsome man at first glance, and yet he possessed a magnetism that drew Cheyenne's gaze a second time. *Tyler Crawford,* some portion of her brain announced, and she knew at once that this was so. He had an intensity about him that she had expected, and though of only medium height he possessed a commanding, riveting presence. It was the eyes, she decided, so blue they seemed unreal and with a directness that both chilled and heated. They stared at her, conveying no message at all, unnervingly robotic, so that she cleared her throat and spoke for no reason other than to escape their spell.

"Hello," she said, as sprightly as she could manage. He nodded, silent and frowning, his craggy face set like stone, his pale mouth turned downward as he moved his eyes over her in deliberate perusal. She opened her mouth again, but he gave her a pointed look, which sent whatever she'd had in mind to say right into oblivion. Then he carefully stepped over, around and through the tangle of her gear, glared chillingly and hurried quietly down the stairs. Cheyenne waited and watched until he'd disappeared around a corner. It occurred to her then that her mouth was still hanging open, and she snapped it shut angrily, spinning around to glare at her own image.

"So," she told it, "that's your new boss." Then she remembered his frown and the coldness of his stare and added, "For the moment." She looked at the clutter on the floor and wondered if it was worth pressing on. Had that look registered immediate and total disapproval, or was she imagining things? She sighed and shook her head and started picking up her gear. Best to get on with it, even if she might be out on her ear by day's end. If he fired her, she'd demand double rate per hour and severance pay. He could, after all, afford it.

The boy's bedroom was on this level. It was not correct to say floor, because the house was broken into many levels, which at first seemed haphazard but later took on a definite pattern and design, achieving the dual purpose of privacy and airy, open, continuity—and all in perhaps two and a half conventional stories. It did, however, make for more stairs, landings and hallways than any person who had ever owned a broom would ever deliberately agree to.

In this particular area the floor was sunbaked terra-cotta tile, decorated at each corner with small, black, stylized figures. Cheyenne swept along the landing, and then left off with the hallway and went into the first room, moving and shaking out the rugs before bringing in the broom. It was a small bedroom, pleasingly furnished with natural pine and decorated with Hopi prints in brown and burnt orange and turquoise blue with touches of sand yellow. A lamp with a pottery base and a few baskets set here and there gave the place an uncluttered but welcoming look. A wicker shade on the window had been raised to let the sunlight filter in through the trees. She liked it. It felt cozy, yet airy, and she could see herself curled up on the full-size bed reading by the light of that lamp with her hand-woven Navaho blanket tucked about her. She cleaned the floors and went on, enjoying her little daydream.

It was the door at the end of the hallway through which Tyler Crawford had made his appearance, so she assumed the room was unoccupied and entered without knocking. She had seen the boy's room the day before, but the house as a whole had so overwhelmed her that she couldn't truly remember what was where, except for the studio loft, which she had been forbidden to enter. It was a surprise then to go through that door and find the boy there, quietly building a wall with locking blocks.

"Oh, excuse me," she said. "I didn't know anyone was in here."

"You're the new maid," he greeted her, looking up with his small, benign face.

"That's right."

He had his father's eyes, she saw, and his mother's dark, shiny hair. The face was round and full, the features as yet unformed, and suddenly they were frowning.

"What day is this?"

"What day?"

"Dust Day? Window Day?"

"Oh." She smiled. "Floor Day. Today's Floor Day."

"Well," he said with a sigh, looking wistfully at his structure, "guess I'd better pick this up, huh?"

"That's okay," she began, fully intent on indulging him. "I can come back later." But he was already dismantling his creation and dumping the blocks in a box.

"Aw, I don't mind. I was getting tired of blocks anyway." He finished his task and put the box away on a shelf in his large, well-organized closet, then crawled onto the bed. "It's okay if I leave my shoes on. I make my own bed."

The little speech was somehow poignant, and she told herself it was unnatural for a four-year-old to be this neat and self-sufficient. She wondered what the punishment would be if he did not maintain such exemplary standards, and it seemed more possible than ever that Tyler Crawford was the ogre that Marilyn feared. She was suddenly very glad she'd agreed to find out the truth. He was an adorable child, and she just knew they were going to get along famously. With that in mind, she decided to start building a few bridges.

"Can I sit down a minute?" she asked, leaving her broom outside the door. He nodded eagerly and drew his little knees up, hugging them. She sat on the corner of his bed. "What's your name?"

"Tyler Royce Crawford, Jr.," he announced proudly. "You can call me Royce."

"Royce it is, then. Nice to meet you, Royce. My name's Cheyenne Cates. You can call me Chey if you prefer."

"I like Cheyenne," he said at once. "That's an Indian name, but you're not an Indian. You've got red hair!"

"Do I?" she teased, pulling a strand down to stare at it cross-eyed. "Well, darned if I don't."

He giggled at that, then informed her importantly that Indians have black hair, mostly. "My friend Eulogio has lots of white in his and some gray, too, but he says even his hair used to be dark as the night when the moon hides."

"And your friend Eulogio is an Indian?"

"He's Navaho, and he's very old, and he paints with sand. I think that's very funny, to paint with sand."

"Well, it's a traditional Native American art form," she started to explain, but he suddenly was more interested in tracing the designs on his bedspread.

"Yes, I know. Is Melly downstairs?"

"Melly?" She found the sudden switch disconcerting.

"Mrs. Mellon. Is she downstairs?"

"Yes, of course, she is."

He started to slide off the bed. "I want to see Melly, and when the floor is dry, I'll come back." He went quickly out of the room, swinging through the door with one hand on the facing. Cheyenne found it unsettling the way he leaped from one subject to another. He seemed to reach out to her, then to draw back quickly and abruptly. Might that be symptomatic of an emotionally abused child?

She brought in her gear and started to clean the floors, first mopping for dust beneath the bed. There were no other pieces of furniture to move away from the walls. Everything had been built in: shelves, drawers, cabinets, even a desk. It was an ideal child's room with a sturdy trundle bed of heavy, golden oak, plenty of area for activity and a bench that also served as a trunk. Heavy braided rugs were scattered over the tiled floor, and these she gently shook and vacuumed and checked for spots before hanging them on the back of the bench while she cleaned the floor.

She had mopped herself right up to the door and was slowly backing through it, the mop swishing back and forth and side to side, when she collided with something warm and solid, and she nearly pitched forward onto the wet tiles. She gave a little scream, and an arm came out and caught her around the middle, pulling her back. Stumbling, she ricocheted off the door frame and spun around, suddenly freed. Tyler Crawford was glaring at her.

"Good heavens, woman! You're going to injure someone!"

"You bumped into me!" she countered hotly, before remembering her professional demeanor. "I mean, excuse me...sir. I didn't know anyone else was around."

She might as well have saved her breath. He wasn't interested in apologies it seemed. "I'm looking for my son. Did you send him away?" The last part had a faintly accusatory inflection to it. Cheyenne stiffened.

"No, I didn't send him away. He was playing when I came in, so I offered to come back later, but he wanted to go see Mrs. Mellon anyway."

"Good enough. I'll go down to the kitchen then." But he didn't. He stayed—and stared. Cheyenne felt her face diffuse with red heat, and as she hated embarrassment, thinking it a weakness, a good deal of anger accompanied it. Her cheeks pulsed with color, violently clashing, she knew, with the orange-red flame of her hair. "What's your name?" he asked abruptly, and she had to gasp a cooling breath before she could answer civilly.

"Cates. Cheyenne Cates."

"*Cheyenne?* Is that your real name?" His tone contained a hint of humor. Her anger canceled all thoughts of maintaining a professional demeanor.

"Of course, it's my real name! Where do you get off asking a question like that?"

"Well, it is rather melodramatic, isn't it?"

"What if it is? It's also different, unique, and I happen to like different and unique."

"So do I—when it's genuine."

"Are you calling me a phony?" she demanded, but to his back. He had turned and was walking swiftly toward the landing.

"If you see my son, tell him it's time for our ride," he called over his shoulder. Cheyenne gaped, and then she threw up her hands, growling through bared teeth.

Marilyn had called him a fiend and an ogre, but the names going through Cheyenne's mind just then were far less polite. In a strange way, though, it was satisfying to find the man lived up to his advance billing. She felt justified and quite brave and, suddenly, fiercely protective of that darling little boy. A measure of her guilt evaporated, and only then could she admit how heavy a load she had felt. The self-righteousness gave her an added boost, so that she went into the next portion of her day with increased vigor, and only much later, when exhausted and sore and alone in her tiny cabaña did she find a moment to feel relief that she hadn't been canned on her first day, after all. But that moment of relief was all she had time for as exhaustion gave way to heavy sleep.

*  *  *

She overslept the next morning and raced out of her bungalow without stockings, slip or hairpins, pulling into the Crawford drive at three minutes after eight. She was yanking a brush through her wild, brick-colored hair—having taken time only to wash her face, brush her teeth and slip on a bra before stepping into her rumpled blue uniform dress and her shoes—when Mrs. Mellon answered the buzzer. She muttered an apology, her heart whumping loudly and rapidly in her ears.

"Never mind, never mind," the housekeeper told her. "Mr. Tyler has asked for you first thing this morning."

Cheyenne's heart stopped. *He's going to can me after all.* The thought came instantly and with dull, dead certainty.

"Put that thing away and come along," Mrs. Mellon was saying. "He'll see you in the sitting room."

"The sitting room," Cheyenne repeated without even the inflection to make it a question.

"Master suite. Go right on up. He's waiting. I took him coffee and a tray of croissants with honey butter, but that won't occupy him long. Mr. Tyler's not one overly interested in his food."

Cheyenne left her bag and brush in the tiny cabinet designated for them and hurried through the laundry room and breakfast nook into the foyer. The sounds of a television and morning cartoons filtered down from the den. With a sense of doom, Cheyenne laid her hand on the brass rail and took the first step. Moments later and slightly breathless, she reached the fourth-level landing and stood before the pegged, cedar-plank door of the master suite, her fist poised above it. Before she could knock, however, the door suddenly opened and Tyler Crawford's electric blue eyes impaled her. He gave her a once-over that was both impersonal and deeply invasive, and she had no doubt that in those three brief seconds he had noted her bare legs, guessed the lack of a slip and concluded that she had hauled herself out of bed only at the last moment, proving her total irresponsibility. Yet, it was her hair upon which his gaze fleetingly lingered.

"Come in, Miss Cates," he instructed brusquely, stepping back. She slipped inside and waited, her heart pounding with almost alarming velocity. "Take a seat, Miss Cates. Coffee?"

She shook her head about the coffee, suddenly aware of how "big" and unruly her hair had become without restraint. She put a hand to it, self-conscious in front of this enigmatic man, and seated herself on the creamy white sofa. Everything in the room was white, from the painted floorboards to the pressed stucco walls to the marble and granite tables and the china lamps. A writing desk took up considerable space along one wall, enameled white and etched with intricate designs. Even the pens in their marble base were white and the terry-cloth robe that hung on a painted bentwood rack beside the door. With some part of her mind she noted that the robe would logically have been better kept in the bedroom, but there were other more important considerations to occupy her at the moment. Impulsively she decided to do something about them.

"Mr. Tyler—I mean, Mr. Crawford—I want to apologize for what happened yesterday. It was my first day and—"

"You can call me Tyler," he said, interrupting.

"What?" She blinked at him, her train of thought abruptly derailed.

"Tyler will do just fine." He had poured himself a cup of coffee and now lowered himself onto a small but comfortable-looking side chair with rolled arms and a low, thick back. Cheyenne still didn't know quite how the conversation had taken this turn or why. She shrugged, her rich, expressive brows drawn together.

"Ah, whatever you—"

"Right." He cut her off again. "Now, Miss Cates, or, um, do you object to my calling you Cheyenne?"

"N-no," she stammered automatically. Then, remembering his derision the day before, she added, "If you can do it with a straight face." It was exactly the wrong thing to say, but she decided that only after she'd said it.

He frowned into his cup. "Only we artists are supposed to be that sensitive, *Miss Cates*."

"And you're so sure I don't belong to the club, aren't you?" she snapped, angry at herself for saying the wrong things and feeling justified at the same time.

He sat back and crossed his legs, white socks showing between sensible black loafers and tan corduroy slacks. It struck her then how effectively his black pullover sweater accented the vivid color of his eyes, and she realized in the same moment that his short, sandy hair was streaked with steel gray. He balanced his cup on his knee and contemplated her for a moment as if she were a laboratory specimen.

"What is your medium?" he said at last, lifting his cup. Both the question and the conclusion had a peculiarly intimate feel. She swallowed, feeling inexplicably shy all at once. She took a deep breath.

"Oil," she admitted. "Sometimes acrylic."

He put down his cup. "So you're a painter."

She lifted her chin haughtily. "That's right."

"Interesting," he muttered, less, it seemed, to her than to himself. "And what do you think of my collection?"

"Astonishing," she answered truthfully, and he nodded with apparent pleasure. "Even the minor pieces are exquisite. I found a tiny Percival White sketch in one of the spare rooms yesterday, and I got so caught up in it I had to skip my afternoon coffee break. The lines of the apple were so deliberate and yet so natural I could almost see the color, you know? What am I saying? Of course you know. You're Tyler Royce Crawford and I'm . . . talking too much.''

"And I'm keeping you from your work," he said quickly, suddenly uneasy. She was thoroughly puzzled, about the conversation, the reason for it, the abrupt change of mood, *changes* of mood. She rose, and he lifted a hand to his eyes as if fighting a sudden ache behind them.

"Would you, um, like me to take the tray down?" she asked.

"No," came the immediate answer. "I mean, yes. That would be fine."

Nodding nervously, she crossed to the table and began gathering up the items that went with the tray. He got up from his chair and brought over his coffee cup, draining away its last contents before placing it on the tray with the other things.

"One other thing, Cheyenne," he said as she lifted it from the table. She looked up. His face was unnecessarily stern. "The uniform," he went on tersely. "Don't wear it again."

Her mouth fell open. "But Mrs. Mellon said—"

"Mrs. Mellon looks quite presentable in an apron," he interrupted. "You look like the proverbial French maid in a bad movie."

The tray landed on the table with a loud, wobbly clatter. "I *what*?"

"I'm not trying to insult you," he shot back, his voice quite loud and commanding.

"Aren't you?" she demanded, digging her fists into the curves of her hips and ready to lambaste him, job or no job.

"Very much the opposite," he replied softly, effectively disarming her. "You are an exotically beautiful woman," he told her. "And I find the uniform distracting, as adolescent as that sounds."

She was speechless, dumbfounded. He found it cynically amusing. "Oh, come now, you must know the effect you have on men, especially men who appreciate natural beauty in all its forms."

Cheyenne closed her mouth and narrowed her light brown eyes. "Well, I was warned about the infamous Crawford charm, but I never would have believed anybody could deliver that line with a straight face."

His blue eyes pinned her, brilliant and sparkling in his craggy, swarthy face. It was a lined and pockmarked face, rugged and uneven and strangely, unconventionally handsome, all bristles from the graying earthen brown of his hair to the silvery glint of a freshly shaven beard already pushing through the thick skin of his angular jaw.

"I don't play with words, Miss Cates. I say essentially what I mean. And as for my 'infamous charm,' as you put it, I think we can attribute that to honesty. People have mixed feelings about honesty. On one hand, they find it refreshing, encountering so little of it. On the other, it discomfits them. Hence the negative connotation attached to a quality all the dishonest people in this world would dearly love to possess. Now if you can't handle blatant honesty, Miss Cates..."

"Oh, I can handle it, *Mr. Crawford, sir*. I can definitely handle it." She folded her arms across her middle and cocked her head to one side, striking a cryptic pose. "And just what would you like me to wear in place of this alluring domestic uniform?"

He worked his jaw from side to side, and she sensed a smile behind the gesture. "Suit yourself," he answered lightly. Then he took an abrupt half step forward, and she felt the flesh beneath her chin warm to his hand. "Just remember," he said, thumb and forefinger curled over her jaw, "I am an intense man, Cheyenne Cates, emotional, passionate, and it has been two long and lonely years since I enjoyed the full companionship of a woman."

Cheyenne's eyes widened. Two years? Could a man as virile, as masculine as this endure two years of celibacy? She had her doubts about that. Still... No one could say she hadn't been warned. At least he had declared himself up front and...honestly. She dropped her gaze, no longer certain her disdain was deserved. Most men, she told herself, grabbed first and made excuses later. Maybe he had only reversed the order, and maybe he was making a sincere attempt to avoid problems. Maybe. She'd give him that much. Just maybe.

Lifting her head up and back, she carefully extricated herself from his grasp. He dropped his hand and moved away.

"You need not make explanations to Mellon," he said, adopting an impersonal tone. "I'll take the tray down myself and settle the matter."

"Then I'll just slip out and run home to change."

"Fine. And, ah..." He lifted a hand, clearly searching for words. He settled for a lame thank-you.

She nodded briskly, waited a moment longer, then turned to hurry away. He stopped her before she reached the door.

"Miss Cates!" She turned back, tilting one brow questioningly. "Cheyenne," he amended awkwardly. Then, with a lift of his shoulders, added, "You're going to do fine here. You're going to do just fine." His voice went soft at the end, conveying warmth and a surprising tenderness. Cheyenne felt a surge of gratitude and friendship toward him, then he scowled and waved a hand imperiously, dismissing her, and she remembered how and why she had come to be here and how miserably predictable the men in her experience had been. If he thought for one moment that he had somehow put her off her guard, she told herself as she hurried away, well, he didn't know her very well or how many men she had dealt with in her lifetime, beginning with her own father.

And this time, she promised herself, trotting rapidly downstairs, she was going to be very, very careful and very, very smart. This time, there was more at stake than the rent or even her pride. A little boy was involved in this, an innocent child, and though some lucky individuals who had never known the scalding effects of mental or physical abuse might reject out of hand the idea that anything could be amiss between this particular son and his father, Cheyenne could not be so sure.

Her own father had been a charming, gregarious man whose friends and neighbors had never witnessed his sudden outbursts of violence and venom. She had taken only a few serious whacks before she had learned to avoid him, and as time went on she had come to disdain his erratic moments of praise as much as his bitter criticism. The worst part of it had been the unpredictability, never knowing what to expect of him in any given situation, and it was that very thing that made her distrust Tyler Crawford: she didn't know what to expect of the man. He was an enigma. She didn't know what to make of him yet, and until she did, she had no intention of letting down her guard. She just wished, she admitted to herself, feeling an odd ripple along her arms, that he wasn't so darned attractive. That was the one thing she hadn't counted on.

"A little hero worship, Cates?" she asked herself cryptically, as she retrieved her purse and slipped past Mellon's wonderfully aromatic kitchen. "The great artist as man? Or is it the other way around?" What was it, she wondered, that made him so compelling? The eyes, of course. They glowed as if they had lights behind them, and yet with color so pure and startling it seemed solid, like chalk locked inside glass, except glass could not carry the kind of warmth she had seen in those eyes. The artist who could properly render those eyes on canvas would be a genius indeed. But beyond the eyes, what was there about him? She mulled that over as she made the drive back down the mountain.

He was of only average height and weight, yet his presence seemed somehow larger than that of other men, and at the same time he seemed compact, as if more muscle than normal had been packed into his light frame. All right, so he seemed unusually fit, she told herself; that still didn't explain the intense aura of masculinity he gave off. That was not physical. It was spiritual or maybe just mental. Maybe it was as simple as a certain adopted attitude, self-confidence, whatever. She couldn't really explain it. She only knew that there was more to it than a craggy face with strong lines and features that weren't particularly handsome in themselves: an angular jaw, a little heavy perhaps, and a rather blunt nose a bit out of line but neither too long nor too short, a smooth brow beneath which the eyes were deeply set and upon which his hairline slightly imposed, a mouth that seemed strangely pale, lips that were a tad thin and gave way to little creases rather than dimples but were expressive nonetheless and well shaped, cheekbones that lacked definition but were aided somewhat by a tiny scar angling downward from the outside corner of his right eye and a pockmark just smaller than the tip of her little finger set high up on the left side. The chin was his best feature. Here was the definition lacking in the bone structure of the upper face: square lines, a slight bulge at the tip that lent prominence to the true dimple above it and bespoke a certain strength, balancing nicely the softness about the eyes.

By the time she reached the bungalow, she had concluded only the obvious: in Tyler Crawford's case, the sum

of the parts definitely seemed greater than the parts themselves. No particular thing about him, save the color of his
eyes, could be said to be extraordinary, yet the total was
most extraordinary indeed. He was, even in the final anal-
ysis, an enigma, a compelling enigma whose allure she must
not allow to overwhelm her.

That in mind, she chose a pair of baggy jeans and a
stained sweatshirt as her new uniform. Her hair she twisted
into a bulky knot at the back of her head, the sides
smoothed and pinned as severely as she could manage. *A
French maid in a B movie, huh?* she thought to herself as she
bundled the navy dress and white apron together. She
straightened and gave herself one last look before starting
back. *Suburban slob,* she decided, satisfied.

"Okay, Mr. Tyler Crawford, get ready to meet your new
domestic, sans the sex appeal." She only wished she could
say the same about her boss, but tried to quell her uneasi-
ness by telling herself to be thankful she still had the job.
After all, he hadn't fired her—not yet, anyway.

Now why wasn't that a comfort?

# Chapter Three

She did not see him again for the remainder of the week. She wore her old jeans and comfortable, roomy tops, her hair wrapped or braided in a knot at the back of her head and stained running shoes with holes in them. Mellon raised a brow but said nothing. Whatever Tyler had told her was enough to quell all but that one tiny show of disapproval. Still, her efforts seemed for naught, with the man completely absenting himself. Apparently Tyler Crawford intended to keep his distance. She was relieved and disappointed, though she denied the last, dusting and scrubbing until her hair escaped its bonds in bouncy, cloudy tendrils and her hands and arms were sore.

The weekend was busy. Cheyenne used her time to clean her own bungalow and do a bit of shopping, while still managing to get in twelve good hours at the easel. Her first check amounted to more than she had expected: Mellon explained that a clothing allowance had been added, as they would not be providing uniforms after all. She said nothing else, and Cheyenne ventured no explanations of her own, but she sensed the older woman's discomfiture, so she went out and spent her clothing allowance on a couple of pairs of bleached cotton bib coveralls, two identical navy blue checked shirts and a half dozen plain white bib aprons. These she augmented with a stack of navy blue bandannas. From now on this would be her uniform.

Mellon approved. She didn't say so, but Cheyenne could feel her relax. Mellon liked things neat and orderly, neater than sloppy jeans and sweatshirts and hair that snaked out in all directions. She looked at the scarf folded and knotted about Cheyenne's long red hair, the clean white apron tied at neck and waist over the prim, checked blouse and sturdy coveralls. Even her cheap sneakers were clean and white. Mellon smiled, and Cheyenne felt she had passed a milestone. She felt better that day, even though Monday was Window Day.

She was working in the living room with a stepladder, a squeegee, a spray bottle of cleaner and a stack of soft towels when Mellon came in with a mug of coffee and an enormous blueberry muffin for her to enjoy during her break. Cheyenne perched on top of her ladder and inhaled the delicious aroma of Mellon's bounty.

"I was thinking I'd take milk and a muffin up to the boy," she said, her hands folded in satisfaction as she watched Cheyenne bite into her puffy pastry.

"Umm." Cheyenne swallowed contentedly. "I'll do it," she volunteered, remembering Mellon's dislike of the stairs. "Soon as I finish my own." The older woman smiled her gratitude and sat down to watch Cheyenne enjoy her goodies. Mellon, it was apparent, liked to see people eat. Cheyenne was suddenly thankful for all those stairs; maybe they would help her keep her figure.

It didn't take her long to have done with her snack. Mellon's warm, sweet muffins were easy to do away with, and her coffee was the very best Cheyenne had ever tasted. Mellon took her cup and saucer back to the kitchen and returned moments later with a red tray bearing the milk and muffin for Royce. Cheyenne climbed the stairs to his room, remembering that she had not so much as glimpsed the boy that day. When she got to his room she knocked, then slowly opened the door. The room was neat and empty. She took the tray to the playroom and then the den, without finding so much as a clue that the boy had even been there. *First the father and then the son,* she remarked silently to herself. These Crawford men had a way of disappearing when it suited them. She set the tray down and left it there, a mild worry beginning in the back of her mind as she started to systematically search the house.

The boy was in none of the spare bedrooms, nor any of the bathrooms. He was not downstairs, and he was not in the family dining room, and no one answered her knock at the master suite sitting room door. That left but one possibility inside the house, and common sense told Cheyenne she had to rule that out before she took her search out of doors. She thought about going back downstairs for Mellon, but her mild worry had grown into a major one, and she didn't want to waste time just because of a silly edict. It wasn't as if she didn't know how to conduct herself in a studio. She was a painter, after all, and what could it hurt to slip quietly in and out?

Swiftly she climbed that last, steep flight of stairs to the attic studio. At the landing she raised her hand to knock, then thought better of it and very gently turned the knob instead. The door silently swung open, and there in the middle of this enormous glass enclave sprawled Royce upon the bare wooden floor, quietly coloring in a fat book of pictures. He looked up as she came through the door and smiled a beatific smile of the innocent.

"Hello," he said, and propped his little chin on the heel of his hand, his feet sparring gently in the air behind his head. Cheyenne laughed. This was one Crawford male she could allow to disarm her.

"What are you doing in here?" she asked, just the faintest note of censure in her voice. He gave her the most sanguine look a boy of four could possibly manage.

"Coloring," he said, turning back to his work. "The light's good for it here." He was so sincere, so definite about it that she had to smile.

"So it is," she replied, allowing herself a look about the room.

It was large and airy with skylights overhead and massive windows that jutted out to a point like the prow of a ship. A vista of forested mountainside filled them, peaceful, silent. She imagined this scene in winter with the snow heavy upon the boughs and blanketing the ground. A fireplace had been built along the wall to the left of the door. The rock was rugged and unpolished, the opening quite grand, certainly sufficient for a child Royce's age to stand up inside. A small couch sat in front of it, the cover faded and worn slick. A fluffy, green-striped blanket was thrown over one arm and trailed down onto the floor where a brown, furry carpet was mounded with square pillows. In their midst sat an empty Chianti bottle and a tray of soiled dishes. *So this,* she thought, *was where Tyler Crawford disappeared to.*

She felt an intense stab of envy, and it took a supreme act of will to keep from looking at the large canvas propped on the cranelike easel in the center of the glass promontory. As a painter, she understood that a work in progress was sacrosanct, and she already felt like a guilty trespasser. She gave the clutter along the remaining wall a cursory glance. There were canvases, paints, easels, palettes and buckets, as well as a sink and cabinets and a door that opened onto what looked like a closet. The oily smell of paint and turpentine mingled with that of wax and charred wood, though it looked as though it had been weeks since a fire had been laid. Cheyenne found it a heady perfume. *Everything,* she thought enviously. *Everything a painter could want.* But she was not that lucky painter. She walked swiftly and lightly across the room and sat down on the floor next to Royce.

"Where'd you get those clothes?" he asked without looking up. Cheyenne frowned. Did she hear the tone of disapproval from a four-year-old?

"I bought them," she answered a bit defensively. "Don't you like them?"

"Yeah. But they're men's clothes, aren't they?"

Great. A four-year-old sexist. "Sometimes men's clothes are more sensible and serviceable than women's clothes, but no, these aren't men's clothes. They just happen to look like men's clothes."

He looked up then and studied her face speculatively. "I like your hair better without that thing on it."

"Oh, do you?" She was getting a bit irritated with the critique. Ever since she'd come into this house someone had been telling her what and what not to wear. "Well, *I* like it better this way. Now you'd better come with me, young man, before you get us both in trouble."

"Why?" he said in that innocently stubborn way of his.

"Because, we're not supposed to be in here. This is your father's place, his very personal, very private work space. Besides, Mrs. Mellon has a blueberry muffin and a glass of milk waiting for you."

"Aw, I'm not hungry right now," he replied, going back to his coloring book. Cheyenne bit her lip.

"Oh, come on now. Don't tell me you can resist Mellon's blueberry muffins. I had one myself a little earlier, and let me tell you, it was scrumptious. Besides, I really don't want your father to find us here."

"And why not, may I ask?" His voice cut through the cavernous room. Cheyenne froze, a sense of doom descending on her like a sledgehammer blow. He stepped out of the closet, which was in reality a bathroom complete with shower as well as shelved storage space. He wore rumpled jeans torn at the knee and a white T-shirt, a brown towel draped about his head and shoulders. He rubbed the water from his bristly hair and swiped the last dab of shaving cream from his dimpled chin. Cheyenne scrambled to her feet, instinctively stepping over the boy, putting herself between them.

"He wasn't hurting anything," she defended instantly, fearing the boy's punishment more than her own. Tyler Crawford smiled, one brow lowered curiously.

"Of course he wasn't. He never does." He pushed the towel off his head onto his shoulders and brought his hands to his hips. Even wet, his hair was bristly, but darker. Cheyenne didn't know quite what to do. She shifted her weight nervously.

"It's all right for him to be here?"

He gave her a sharp look. "This is his home. Why wouldn't it be all right for him to be here?"

"Well, Mellon said—"

"Yes, yes." He seemed impatient. "Mellon is a little frightened of the place. She doesn't quite understand what goes on here. She cleaned a palette for me once."

"Oh, no."

"I'm afraid I yelled at her. It took hours to get the second mix right without the first to compare it with. Since then she's given the place a wide berth."

"I thought you were the one who declared it forbidden territory."

Another sharp look, followed by a wide, quick smile. "You've heard about Tyler Crawford the ogre, have you? Well, I have a temper, but—" he stooped and lifted the boy off the floor "—I wouldn't be so foolish as to deprive myself of the company of my son." He tapped the boy's chin with a loose fist. "No room is forbidden him in his own home." The child wrapped both arms and legs about his father.

"Mellon has blueberry muffins," he said.

"Is that so?" replied Tyler. "And I suppose you want some, eh?"

"Yes. Can we have them here?"

"I don't see why not."

"Do you know," the boy inquired most seriously, playing with his father's spiky hair, "that she has an Indian name?"

Tyler sent her a measured glance. "Yes, well, she's a very interesting lady."

"Can I have pants like those?"

The question caught Cheyenne off guard, and she had to laugh, looking down at herself. Tyler controlled a smile, and his eyes slid over her, impassive yet strangely probing.

"I think we can arrange that, so long as you don't ask for the apron, too."

The boy wrinkled his nose, taking the admonition most seriously. "No way!" he declared.

"You object to the apron?" Cheyenne asked, more of the father than the son.

"No. I object to the scarf," he replied coolly, and her brows went skyward, along with her hands. "Never mind. Would it be too much to ask you to bring up the muffins?

I've promised Royce a lesson, and if we don't get started soon, I'll get nothing accomplished on my canvas today.''

Cheyenne was already backing toward the door. "No problem. What would you like to drink? Coffee?''

"Cola!" Royce shouted, eliciting a stern glower from his father.

"We'll both have milk," Tyler ordered in a low voice, and as Cheyenne exited she heard him say, "Now, young man, what have I told you about drinking too many colas?" She wanted to stay and hear more, fearing that the infamous Crawford temper was about to rear its ugly head at last, but what could she do? If she interfered, he would fire her, and then who would keep an eye on the boy? Better to simply hurry back and try to forestall with her presence any incorrect behavior.

She sprinted the stairs, completely forgetting the tray she had left earlier in the den. Mellon gasped and clucked her tongue when Cheyenne swept breathlessly into the kitchen and requested another tray. "What are you about, child?" she called after her as she snatched the hastily filled tray and rushed from the room. Cheyenne didn't even attempt a reply. What could she say? *This man intrigues me, and I can't wait to get back to him,* or *I have to know for sure that the boy is safe?* It wouldn't have made sense to Mellon. How could it when it didn't make sense to her? But then it was her job, her *mission* to make sense of it. How could she explain that to Mellon?

As she climbed the many stairs, more slowly this time with two full glasses of milk threatening to spill over, she thought about what she was doing, about the bright and sweetly precocious little boy and the man who forbade his aunt even an innocent visit. The kid was adorable, apparently normal if you overlooked a rather obsessive neatness, and yet there was something else about him that disturbed her, a moodiness, a silence. It was the same thing that disturbed her about the father. Like her own father, he was unpredictable, mercurial, with a kind of leashed power that she had learned early on to fear. But was it the same?

She thought of Tyler Crawford smiling down at his son, lifting him into his arms. She thought of little Royce wrapping his whole body about his father in an eager embrace. They had seemed so loving in that moment—but then she thought of her own father praising a drawing she had done, seeming so proud and pleased, then destroying it later in a fit of temper, punishment for arriving late for dinner, or rather, later than he. She remembered what he'd said as he slowly tore the paper down the middle: "Now then, young lady, what have I told you about being on time?" She quickened her pace, and milk dribbled down the outside of the glasses.

They were sitting on the edge of the sofa when she entered the room. Royce held a large sketch pad in his lap, one arm bracing it. In his hand was a thick pencil with which he was making broad, confident strokes one would not expect from a child. Cheyenne approached carefully, taking a circuitous route that brought her near the back of the couch. What she saw stunned her. Tyler looked up then and followed her with his eyes, a small, almost wistful smile on his lips. She moved around the end of the sofa and set the tray on the serving table, then picked up the table and set it, tray and all, in front of the sofa.

"Look at this," Tyler said to her; then to the boy, "You've done very well. Now have your muffin." The boy slid off the sofa onto the floor, relinquishing the sketch pad and reaching for the treat. Cheyenne moved to Tyler's side, sitting when he moved over to allow her room. Still, it was a tight squeeze, and she was very aware of him, fresh and clean from his shower and utterly masculine there next to her, the drawing in his own hands now. "Have you ever seen anything like this?" he asked in a soft voice. Cheyenne craned her head to view the drawing more clearly. It was a rooster's head, done with a minimum of strokes and shaded expertly, the lines thickening and darkening in exactly the right places to give it depth and dimension.

"Remarkable," she murmured. "He did it just now? So quickly?"

Tyler nodded gravely and with his fingers retraced the lines. "We were working on shading. Look at this. Here. Here. And this he did entirely on his own, without a word from me."

"Remarkable," she said again.

"Genius," he replied proudly, keeping his voice low. "True genius." He ruffled his son's dark hair, and the boy smiled back at him with a mouth crammed to overflowing with blueberry muffin. "You know better than that, Royce. Take smaller bites." The boy nodded, eyes large as if they, too, were overstuffed. Cheyenne was still smiling down at him when Tyler shoved the sketch pad into her lap.

"Now," he said, giving it a nudge so that the corner of the pad poked her in the thigh, "it's your turn. Let's see what sort of an artist you are, Cheyenne Cates."

She stared at him. He was deadly serious, his blue eyes waiting, challenging. She blinked thoughtfully, then slowly pulled the pad from his grasp.

"All right." Challenge accepted.

He compressed his mouth into a sort of grin and proffered the fat pencil. She took it, folded the paper back, glanced at the fresh sheet and began to draw without thinking. Only when the first few strokes were on paper did she realize what she was doing, but then it was too late. She had begun and she would finish. She worked furiously, slashing the paper with dark, hurried strokes. It was rough and un-

flattering, all crags and bristles and creases. When she got
to the mouth, she was tempted to look at him, but pride
made her search her mind instead, and she found she had
stored away a surprisingly accurate and detailed picture of
him. She bent to the work, forgetting momentarily that he
was there, waiting and watching, judging her.

Several minutes passed. Absently she lifted a hand and
swept the scarf from her head, needing freedom and light-
ness. She shook her head and wet the tip of her finger with
her tongue, smoothing it over the paper to smudge the heavy
pencil strokes. A moment longer and she tackled the eyes,
biting her lip and bending low over the paper as her fingers
fashioned the image in her mind. Her hair fell over her face,
and she tossed it away with a jerk of her head and a flip of
her fingers, but she was engrossed, and a second or two later
it came tumbling down again. She raised a hand to push it
aside, almost finished now, and then felt it magically lifted
away. She looked up and at the same time felt the brush of
his fingertips against the side of her neck. The shock was
electric and hot, flashing through her, searing nerve endings. She held her breath, waiting for the fingertips to with-
draw, feeling instead the full weight of his hand as it rested
on the back of her neck beneath the curtain of her hair. She
was sure he could feel her pulse there; her heart was rock-
eting off like fireworks.

Those blue eyes confronted her, bright and inquisitive,
studying, probing. She couldn't bear them. Her heart would
explode if she allowed them to linger on hers. Nervously she
bent back to her work, trying hard to concentrate, breathing roughly through her mouth, but the work was done. She
could add only delicate shadings and superfluous marks.
Pride finally forced her to stop, pride and a full sense of
herself as an artist. She laid the pad on her lap and held the
pencil in her fist without looking up. The hand at last moved

away, coming down to take the pencil from her grasp. A kind of rebelliousness flushed her, the sort she'd felt as a child when she'd both wanted and not trusted the touch of her father. She lifted her head and gazed boldly into his eyes. She shoved the drawing toward him, and he tugged his eyes away to look at it.

For a long moment he stared, and then he took the sketch pad into his hands and held it up, studying it critically. A terrible confusion assaulted her. She both wanted and feared his critique. It occurred to her guiltily that this was what she was really here for, that all those other lofty notions were but excuses—and yet, she hadn't really expected anything like this to happen. At most, she'd expected to slip around in the background, peering over the great man's shoulder, absorbing some tiny secret of technique from a safe and anonymous distance. She was holding her breath again.

"It's very good," he said at last. "Quite mature."

She felt the grin lifting the corners of her mouth. "Do you really think so?"

"Don't be coy," he said, handing it back to her and reaching for his milk glass. "You know what you're doing, what you're capable of." She bristled. He gulped the milk, wiping away the inevitable mustache with his hand. "But it always helps to have someone else say it, doesn't it?" He smiled and she felt the defensiveness drain away.

"Can I look?" The boy's small voice seemed to push everything back toward normalcy. Tyler took him on his lap and showed him the drawing. "That's you!" he giggled, twisting about to tug a sprig of his father's hair reflected perfectly in the portrait.

"Yes, indeed. Cheyenne seems to have quite a talent for portraiture."

The child leaned across and linked an arm about her neck. "Can I have it?" He knew too well, this Crawford man, how to get what he wanted.

"Of course you may," she replied happily, and he put a crumby kiss on her cheek.

"Run on now," his father told him, "and take your things with you, and don't forget to thank Cheyenne for bringing our snack or Mellon for making it."

She got another blueberry kiss, on her chin this time as his aim was spoiled by the act of sliding off his father's lap. "You're welcome," she called after him as he ran out, leaving her alone with his father.

"I predict," Tyler said at once, "that the time will come when I am known simply as the father of Tyler Royce Crawford, Jr. He has the natural talent of a Mozart."

"But you haven't told him that," she commented pointedly. He stretched his arms out along the back of the sofa.

"I always praise his work or, rather, his play, for that's what it is to him, and that's what it should remain until such a time as he chooses otherwise. He should paint because painting is life to him, not because I have given him to understand that I expect it or even hope for it. Talent is a random happening. Its utilization is a matter of choice. But art, artistic expression, is an obsession that won't let go. When and if it takes hold of him, I will know, and then I'll press, then I'll let words like 'child prodigy' fall happily from my proud lips."

The tone was teasing, humorous, but the underlying message was well thought out and seemed sincere. She decided once again he deserved at least the benefit of the doubt, and it occurred to her that this was quickly becoming a pattern with her. That thought brought a tinge of color to her cheeks and a heightened awareness of his arm skimming her shoulders. All at once she wanted to get out of there.

"I ought to be getting back to work," she began, but as she got up, he did, too. Then, as casually as he set his glass aside, he took her hand.

"I'd be interested in your opinion," he said, leading her toward the large canvas standing on the spindly legs of its easel in the focal point of the room. "Turnabout is fair play, after all."

Her previous curiosity bobbed to the surface like a freed cork, creating eddies and waves that radiated through her, tingling and expectant. She felt herself tugged along, her reluctance canceled out by her anticipation. This was a privilege, she knew, probably a rare one, to view a work in progress by one of the most critically acclaimed artists of the time. She stepped before the canvas with reverent timidity, the great vista of the moutainside at her back, her hand warm in his. For a brief moment, it seemed their altar, they, a couple, standing before their deity as one, but then she allowed her eyes to see the piece, to take it in as a whole, and suddenly the experience became an individual one, separate, private. The color hit her first: white washed over a field of cerulean blue, the blue reduced, or rather, heightened, to a feeling, an emotion. And such a blue! A blue unlike itself. Not the blue of despair or dread or depression, but the blue of brightness and warmth, sunshine and wellbeing, order and promise and beauty. It was ethereal, the blue of an Eden found only in emotion, in spirit.

Upon that field of blue, for that's what it was, a field, a meadow at the edge of a forest, dappled with flowers and coaxed by rills and pretty stones, stood a woman. She was a woman not in detail but in spirit. Not a wraith, for she was more substantial than that, but a woman somehow apart, a woman surpassing mere physical presence. Her face was not visible, but she had long hair—she could not tell what color—and graceful limbs and a slender neck and long, delicate fingers that were lifted in a gay, carefree trill of goodbye. How she knew it was goodbye the woman signaled, she could not have said. She only knew that as she skipped across that fair, blue field she went toward something, eager and happy, and bade farewell to something else.

It was all right there for the eye to see, and yet obscured by that icy white overwash. It was as if that something to which the woman in the painting bade farewell was on the other side of a thick veil or perhaps a wall of ice. It was hard to tell what that obstruction was, and yet the viewer was held within its realm and clearly not released into the other. It was here that the painting yet needed work, and she felt certain that one day soon its meaning would be fully rendered, though she could not begin to guess how. Even in its present state, however, the effect was both heartening and chilling and ultimately nothing less than masterful.

"Incredible," she whispered, without even knowing she had done so, and it was then that she felt his hand caress the cloud of her hair. As before, electricity jolted through her, the air stopping in her lungs.

"Yes," he said softly, "incredible," and the certain knowledge that he was speaking of her shocked as profoundly as his touch, paralyzing her body and mind, so that she froze, her thought processes grinding to an abrupt halt. Even her heart seemed to have stopped. Then suddenly everything went into fast forward.

The hand that caressed her hair now invaded it, cupping the back of her head, while the other appeared just above her waist, turned her and slid around to the small of her back, pulling her toward him. She felt the small collision as their bodies met, and all at once her heart was pulsing like a water cannon. There was a moment, just a part of a moment before his mouth came down on hers, when she knew she could stop it—and didn't—and then it was too late.

His mouth came down hard, fit hers to itself and plundered, its manipulations so intense, so forceful that her entire body seemed to react as if by command. Where there had been paralysis before there was now a stunning clamoring, a melting and warming, a vast, deepening yearning. She had never felt anything like it before, never even sensed that this kind of need lay buried within her. She was at once alarmed, intrigued and appalled as the kiss simply burgeoned and blew apart, sending them reeling away from one another.

Her hand went instinctively to her mouth, and hot tears started in her eyes. She couldn't think, and she couldn't believe she had allowed this to happen, now, of all times, of all men. She'd slapped men for less, given up jobs, suffered the utmost indignation, and all she could do at this moment was tremble.

"Well," he commented cryptically, quoting, "She had one failing..."

The obvious criticism stung her sharply. That damnable blush burned her cheeks, and it was in her mind to finish it for him and defend herself with, "Had a woman ever less?" Instead she heard herself saying, "She isn't the only one."

He gave her one burning and deadly glare and turned his back. "I expected passion in a woman like you, an artist."

"I expected decency."

She waited a moment, steeling herself against the rage she saw in the lift and fall of his shoulders, the stiffness of his stance, the arms held tight against his sides, the hands knotted into fists. But he said not a word, made no move, only stared into his framed forest through the cold wall of glass, until she realized that she had been dismissed, sent away, banished.

She wanted to strike him, to hurt him somehow. For a moment she indulged herself in the idea of doing so. She saw herself in her mind, running forward and beating her fists against the hard wall of his back, feeling the softness of the white cotton give way to the solid muscle beneath and that give grudgingly as her blows fell. Then her mind took the drama one step further, and she saw him turn and engulf her in his arms, quelling her terror—for it was terror, not anger on her part—and subduing her with tender, ardent kisses that made joy of her pain and passion of her fear. She thought of them coming together like warring lovers, and suddenly she was more frightened that it wouldn't happen than that it would. She gasped, so confused the very confusion itself was painful. She felt lost. She was that little girl again feeling the euphoria of her father's pride and praise and, simultaneously, the searing depth of his rejection and criticism. And so she did what she had always done: she ran.

He took the scarf that billowed out of his back jeans pocket, her scarf, and with a small, underhanded toss, deposited it in her path. She snatched it up, taking it to mean that she should cover her hair again, make herself less desirable again. She was working furiously at the knot as she shouldered her way through the door, tears coursing down her cheeks. Outside on the landing she mopped her face mechanically with the scarf, then finished untying it, her fingers trembling. She folded it and threw it over her head, catching a sizable hank of hair in the new knot she made, wondering all the while what was happening to her, how she came to be here, what she must do. Then by simple rote she descended the stairs, and by sheer habit she pulled herself together and returned to her work, thinking and not thinking, feeling and not feeling in the same confused eternity that became her day, until she could almost convince herself that the kiss hadn't happened at all and that if it had it meant nothing to her. Nothing.

# Chapter Four

I don't know, Marilyn." Cheyenne paced the floor in front of her old classmate's garish desk. It was late, and the shop was closed, but Marilyn had agreed to meet with her, and this seemed the safest place. "Things just aren't working out like I thought they would," she went on, remembering how Tyler had skulked about the house that day, glaring at her whenever their paths had crossed, muttering to himself about the inconvenience of vacuum hoses and mop pails. It had been a long, tense day, and tomorrow was bound to be another.

Marilyn crossed her lean legs, pressed her blood-red fingertips to her temples and leaned back in her chair. "He's won you over," she observed with narrowed eyes. "He's too smart for you. He probably read you the first day, and ever since then he's been showing you exactly what you want to see."

"Don't be absurd. He doesn't suspect a thing. How could he?"

"I never said he suspected a connection between the two of us. Believe me, if he did, you'd be out on your ear the very next moment. I said that he knows how to impress a woman, how to get next to her, and he's gotten next to you, hasn't he?" Cheyenne rolled her eyes, but inside she was trembling. "Are you going to tell me what happened, what changed your mind?" Marilyn asked. "Something has."

"No," Cheyenne said, a little too quickly perhaps. "I haven't changed my mind. It's just that I never had an opinion one way or another, and I still don't. You see, I had expected to have made up my mind by now. I expected to know by now if Tyler Crawford is all the things you said he was or not, but I don't. That's the problem, Marilyn, I just don't know if what I'm doing is right or not."

"Oh, God," Marilyn groaned, and rocked back in her chair. "That darling little boy all alone there with that moody, maniacal man, and you just don't know if protecting him is right or not."

"Cut it out, Stucky!" Cheyenne warned in a taut voice. "All I'm saying is that Tyler Crawford isn't showing his hand, one way or the other. I just haven't seen any real evidence that the boy is being mistreated."

"All right," Marilyn countered, snapping back into a sitting position. "Let's just go over the last two weeks in detail. Mellon hired you right off. She told you never to go into the studio. Tyler saw you the next day and seemed displeased. You met the boy. He impressed you as being a bit withdrawn and—" Marilyn daintily rubbed her nose, and Cheyenne suspected she was hiding a smirk "—too neat. Day two, Tyler summons you to a formal conference, during which he tells you not to wear your uniform anymore. Curious that, but never mind. You don't see Tyler for several days. Then on Monday you find the boy in the studio. You figure he's in trouble, the studio being off limits according to Mellon, but Tyler says it isn't so. In your presence he gives the boy an art lesson. Turns out the kid is a prodigy of some sort, but Tyler doesn't want to push him. Now you tell me the kid's spending hours a day drawing and coloring and you and Mellon are pinning his little masterpieces all over the house and that even though his only parent has locked himself away, he's happy as a lark. Now that right there tells me the kid's happiest when he doesn't have to deal with his father. But you're not sure."

"*You* want to believe the worst!" Cheyenne argued, rolling her hands into fists atop Marilyn's desk. Marilyn stood up very slowly, very regally.

"I have to believe the worst," she said evenly. "My nephew's welfare is at stake."

Something very like shame filled Cheyenne. She dropped her gaze guiltily. Yes, of course. It was better to err on the side of the boy's best interests. She took a deep breath, knowing she was going to go back into that house and to keep going back until she was sure, really sure. All she had to do, she told herself, was stay away from Tyler Crawford and concentrate on his son. She could do that, couldn't she?

Marilyn walked around the end of her desk, arms folded. "Why did he ditch the uniform?" she asked unexpectedly.

Cheyenne tried to stay cool. She attempted a nonchalant shrug. "Guess he didn't like it."

"Or liked it too much."

Betraying color flooded Cheyenne's cheeks. She hated her propensity to flush, hated it with a passion, and she turned her back on Marilyn, hoping to deny the obvious. She failed, of course. Marilyn came around quickly to face her.

"What'd you do, unbutton it down to the waist? Hike up the hem? Honey, you're playing with fire here. Tyler Crawford is not the sort of man you can flirt with or play with, believe me! He's dangerous. He's—"

"How dare you!" She was angry, as angry with herself as with Marilyn, and therefore incautious. "I've never enticed a man in my life! *He* made the pass at me!"

Marilyn snorted derisively. "I've heard of women who couldn't resist a man in uniform but never the other way around! I mean, it's ridiculous."

"I couldn't agree more. Now can we just drop it?"

Marilyn's artfully drawn brows went up as she studied her. "Not until you tell me the rest of it."

Cheyenne looked away, nostrils flaring as she remembered the incident. For a moment she considered lying, but she'd never been very good at that sort of thing. What difference did it make anyway? She made a flippant gesture. "He kissed me, all right?"

Marilyn's mouth fell open. She was utterly speechless for several seconds. Then slowly the red lips formed themselves into a bitter smile. "I hope you didn't take it seriously."

"Oh, don't worry!" Cheyenne snapped. "I didn't measure up to expectations."

Marilyn's smile became one of thinly concealed triumph, and for the first time Cheyenne wondered if her unlikely coconspirator had once herself harbored unconfessed feelings for her enigmatic brother-in-law. Was there more here, she wondered, than concern for a young nephew?

"It's just that I don't want to jeopardize—"

"Yes, I'm sure," Cheyenne cut her off.

"Really, Cheyenne," Marilyn went on cattily. "I don't know what this fatal attraction of yours is, but take my advice and steer clear of Tyler Crawford. This is one employer you can't handle by slapping his face in public. Remember how my dear sister ended up and what you're there for."

"And you remember that I'm doing you a favor by being there at all!"

Marilyn cooled her gaze. "Yes, of course. Now, has my nephew mentioned me? Does he ever ask for me? We were so close once." She said this last with such wistfulness that Cheyenne almost believed her. Almost, but not quite, and never completely again.

"No one's mentioned you," she said coldly, and it did not escape her notice that Marilyn seemed oddly unaffected by the news. But no matter. It was the boy who concerned her, the boy and only the boy. Or so she wanted to believe.

Going back to work Wednesday morning was one of the most difficult things Cheyenne had ever done, and yet there was a comforting familiarity about it. She'd developed, she realized, something of a routine. She went in and put away her things, then slipped into the kitchen for a cup of Mellon's good coffee and a hot biscuit with little bits of spicy sausage baked inside. Mellon smiled at her and chatted about the weekend and her sons. The one with the girl was getting married after all, and Cheyenne could tell she was excited about that. It made her feel warm inside to think that people really could fall in love, overcome obstacles, get married, and everyone would be happy about it. Well, maybe not everyone; the girl's father was accepting but not thrilled, according to Mellon.

"But just wait," she said knowingly, "until the grandbabies start arriving. He'll change his tune then."

Cheyenne automatically thought of Royce. Had anyone been thrilled about that little boy? "Kids should have grandparents," she said, adding offhandedly, "Are Mr. Crawford's parents living?"

Mellon shook her head. "Not Mr. Crawford's nor Mrs. Crawford's, God rest her."

"So there's no other family, then?" Cheyenne asked carefully. Mellon's gentle face hardened.

"None worth mentioning," she stated tersely.

"How sad," Cheyenne murmured, wondering why Mellon's expression had changed. Did Mellon dislike Marilyn, and if so why? Was it just that Tyler disliked her, or was it something else, something more? She had to consider the possibility that Marilyn was not the bereaved, concerned auntie she pretended to be, but not just now. It was Dusting Day, and she had noticed several particularly cobwebby places while doing the floors the day before. She would need the stepladder and the feather duster in addition to a soft cloth, wood polish . . . She ticked off several other items in her head, visualizing the articles to be cleaned as she took leave of Mellon's cozy kitchen.

It was good to be busy, and as the morning wore on she realized with some relief that she hadn't encountered Tyler even once. Her luck ran out around lunchtime, though, when she was carefully cleaning several small pieces of statuary displayed in a curio cabinet on the third-level landing. He came out of his bedroom door and rushed along the landing, brushing past her while throwing on a banded, dark brown jacket of soft leather. The weather had been cool for several days now, and already the mountainside was dappled with gold and copper. Soon it would be ablaze, and soon after that the first snow would fall. All this came to her as she tried, unsuccessfully, not to watch him descending the stairs. She gently wiped the alabaster gentleman in her gloved hands, allowing herself a final glance at the stairway in time to catch him looking up at her. She had caught him in the act of turning up his collar. It gave him a decidedly rakish look, and she realized for the first time that he was truly handsome in a rugged, unconventional way. He brought his arms down, his gaze holding hers for just a fraction of a second longer, then he turned and went swiftly on his way. She wondered irritably where he was going and when he would return, then reminded herself that it was none of her business and concentrated on being relieved to have him out of the way.

When he had not returned by quitting time, however, she found herself wondering again where he had gone, and then she thought of Royce and wondered if he would have to pass the evening alone with only Mellon to keep an eye on him from her kitchen. She decided to look in on him herself and remembered that she had seen him watching afternoon cartoons in the den earlier. He was still there, curled up in a big chair, his chin supported by a throw pillow he hugged to his chest. The early news was playing.

Cheyenne felt a pang of sympathy for him. He looked small and lonely and bored. She went over and let her fingers stroke his dark hair. He looked up with a ready smile and blinked his enormous eyes at her.

"What's the stock market?" he asked. Cheyenne disciplined a smile.

"It's a very grown-up and very expensive game. Men and women who should know better gamble huge amounts of money and shout at one another. It's very complicated and very serious, and to tell you the truth I don't understand it very well myself."

"Can you play it on the telephone?" he queried.

Cheyenne nodded. "Yes, you could say that."

He turned back to the television. "I think Dad plays."

"Does he?" Cheyenne found that interesting. "Is that where he's gone, to see his broker?"

He gave her a blank look. "No, he's gone to see Terri and Eulogio."

"Eulogio," she said. "Isn't that your Indian friend?"

"Umm-hmm."

"And who is Terry?"

"She's Daddy's agent," he answered matter-of-factly. *She?* Cheyenne felt a strange fluttering in her chest. She had to swallow before she could speak.

"Why didn't you go with him?" she managed to say. "I know how you like Eulogio."

He made a face and looked at her. "I don't like Terri. She always says, 'Don't touch! Don't touch!' and it always makes Dad mad when she does it, so I just don't go."

That pleased her, not only that Tyler took offense at his son being scolded but that Royce didn't like her. She was able to smile. "Well, don't take it personally," she told him. "Some people just don't like kids, and I think that's kind of sad, don't you?"

He grinned up at her, wrinkling up his little nose. "You like kids, don't you?"

She grinned back and tapped the end of that cute nose. "Yes, I do. I especially like smart little boys with dark hair and sweet faces."

He giggled. "I like ladies with long red hair."

"Well, aren't we in luck!" she declared, dropping down on the arm of the chair to tickle him. He laughed and kicked and seemed so suddenly happy that she couldn't help feeling that way herself. It was just then that Mellon appeared, her plump hands folded over her apron.

"Listen to the two of you," she said, "having a grand old time. Dinner's almost ready, Royce. You'd best wash up now."

The boy bounced onto the floor obediently. "Can Cheyenne stay for dinner, Melly?" he asked as he skipped toward the door. *"Please,"* he added, swinging on the doorknob. Mellon looked at Cheyenne beseechingly.

"There's plenty, and the boy could use the company. Me, I'm so tired I just want to soak my feet and go to bed."

Cheyenne smiled at Royce. Why not? It was an opportunity to really get to know the boy, and with Tyler away the timing was propitious.

"I'd love to stay," she answered. "Thank you."

"Wahoo!" the boy yelped. "Can we play a game?"

Cheyenne laughed. "Sure we can."

"I bet I can beat . . ." The rest was lost as he ran to wash up.

"He probably can, too," Mellon said with a laugh. "But maybe you'll be more of a challenge than I am."

Cheyenne smiled and nodded, but she was thinking, *Poor child, relying on the kindnesses of servants and strangers.* But then it wasn't exactly true, she reflected fairly. She was no longer a stranger, and Mellon was treated more like a member of the family than a domestic. Still, it did seem a shame. Maybe Marilyn was right, after all. Then again . . . Oh, it was all so confusing, and she suddenly realized she didn't want to think about it anymore. The boy needed her. That was all that mattered at the moment.

The evening was most pleasant. Royce was wonderful company, intelligent, charming, engaging. He kept her soundly entertained with his bright, cheery chatter, and she could tell that he was enjoying her company. She was his personal audience, his own private gallery, and he played straight to her with an eagerness she had little trouble labeling as loneliness, increased, she was certain, by an insensitive parent. The meal itself seemed rather subdued in comparison to their play before and afterward, but then again Mellon's chicken potpie was good enough to capture anyone's full attention, especially when accompanied by a cold glass of creamy white milk and a platter of cheese and fruit. She watched the boy pick his fruit with judicious solemnity, three plump grapes, three slices of crisp apple, a quarter of a pear, which he cut into three equal pieces. She had fun just watching him.

It was later, though, that he really shone. He talked non-stop for thirty solid minutes about a children's movie he'd seen on television, giving her details of the action and snippets of conversation in different voices. She didn't understand a word of it, had not the foggiest notion what it was about or what had gone on, but she enjoyed his rendition, nonetheless. After that performance he pulled out a collection of strange-looking vehicles and began twisting them into even stranger robots. This was done with appropriate sound effects and a swiftness that left her once again in total confusion. She worked unsuccessfully on the one he gave her while he transformed ten or twelve others. After a bit he grew impatient with her clumsiness and took it from her, adeptly twisting and snapping until it became a grinning head which he joined with other newly created body parts to form one large, formidable robot. She sat by, transfixed, and pretended to contribute to the scenario by growling and screeching at random, while he put the robots through their paces. In the space of an hour they created a war, fought it and negotiated an acceptable peace that left everyone friends and good guys.

It was Mellon who suggested that it was time for calmer activities, but it was Cheyenne who suggested the story. She had intended to read one of his choice, but he begged her to "pretend" one, to tell a story of her own devising. It was a challenge to which she felt unequal, but once he had curled up in her lap and turned up that eager little face she discovered an untapped reserve of imagination and enthusiasm within her.

She chose as her protagonist a lizard whom she called Ebenezer and spun him into a story of tragedy turned miracle when he lost his tail and grew another. The boy's rapt attention was all she needed to tell her that she was doing well, and when he clapped and giggled at the end she felt enormous satisfaction and pride.

They both greeted the announcement of bedtime with a mixture of resignation and regret. To her joy, he pleaded with Mellon for a little more time, the response to which was the suggestion that perhaps Cheyenne would stay to help him with his bath and tuck him in. She agreed readily and prepared a warm, soothing tub while he laid out his pajamas and clean undershorts. He told her she was supposed to watch him brush his teeth, which she did with an intensity of attention a microsurgeon would have appreciated. While he bathed, she turned down his sheets and straightened his room, what there was to straighten. The boy was uncommonly neat and organized and, she told herself, astoundingly brilliant. Was this, she wondered, what it felt like to be a parent? She was a bit frightened by the combination of emotions, the protectiveness, the pride, the sheer joy, this nameless, niggling fear that something—anything—might go wrong in this delightful little person's life.

He didn't waste much time drying after his bath, and her expected examination was a wet, clammy one, but she pronounced him clean behind the ears and on the back of his neck and then went to wipe up his wet, slippery path. By the time she'd finished, he was all dressed and sliding between the sheets. He gave her a protracted, "Ah," and she smiled down at him. He held up his arms for a hug and a goodnight kiss, with which she delightedly supplied him.

"Will you stay tomorrow night, Cheyenne?" he asked, his arms about her neck.

"We'll have to see about that," she answered evasively, her heart twisting. He lay back, and she ruffled his hair and wished him a final good-night. She got up to go, reluctantly, gently, and then she turned away. Tyler Crawford stood in the doorway, filling it with his compact, controlled presence. She sucked in her breath, their eyes locked, and Royce shouted a happy, "Dad!"

Tyler laughed and dropped his gaze simultaneously. Cheyenne stepped aside as he brushed past her, feeling at once displaced and envious. She heard rather than saw the greeting they shared: the laughter, the smacks of kisses and the grunts and rustles of hugs, the tickling and more laughter, the apologies for being late, the brief but funny description of Terri and Eulogio's meeting.

"Is she going to help Eulogio?" the boy asked.

"I think so," Tyler responded. "She's pompous and disagreeable, but she knows talent when she sees it, and Eulogio's got it."

"Yeah," the boy agreed. Then his voice brightened. "Hey, I bet Terri would help Cheyenne, too!"

It was those words that made her turn, made her see what was really taking place here, a loving father and a loving son connected by trust and commitment and coming together again after dealing, each in his own way, with the little duties and unpleasantries of life. She became aware of their eyes on her, realized that they were staring back. She shifted self-consciously and managed a smile.

"Oh, I don't think Terri would want to bother about someone like me," she said lightly, but Royce's little face set stubbornly.

"Yes, she would. I could show her the sketch you made me of Dad."

"I imagine Cheyenne has even better works to show," Tyler commented, settling his son into his bed once more. He smoothed the covers beneath the boy's chin. "Now is not the time to discuss it, though. You have to get to sleep."

The boy smiled, the matter instantly dismissed. "Cheyenne stayed with me tonight," he said. "Cheyenne's my best friend."

"Truly?" Tyler seemed neither displeased nor surprised. "Well, what a lucky boy you are."

"She made up a story about a lizard!" the boy went on.

"A lizard? Oh, my, she is a remarkable woman then. Maybe she'll stay with you again another time."

"Yes, I'd like that," Cheyenne agreed quickly, wondering if the offer was genuine.

Royce held out his arms to her again, and she maneuvered herself awkwardly past Tyler, twisting her upper torso and pulling in her elbows to keep from touching him while she hugged his son. The final hug belonged to Tyler, though, and he made it a joyful one. Satisfied, the boy then simply rolled over, tucked his hands beneath his cheek and started off to dreamland, a look of utter peace on his cherubic face.

Tyler adjusted the lights in the room, then they went out into the hallway, gently closing the door behind them. Cheyenne put some distance between them and rubbed her upper arms, suddenly chilled.

"Thank you," he said stiffly as they started to move toward the landing. "I hate to leave him. Mellon takes good care of him, but entertaining him seems to take more energy than she has these days."

"Oh, but I didn't entertain him," she hurried to amend. "Quite the contrary. *He* entertained me."

Tyler smiled and hung his thumbs in his waistband, elbows tucked up high and behind him. "Yes, I can believe that. He can be such good company at times that it's easy to forget how small and dependent he really is."

"I think I know what you mean," she replied, hugging herself.

He stopped, and she felt compelled to stop alongside him. "Do you?" He shook his head. "Unless you've had someone like him in your life, someone so trusting, so completely focused, so unshakably loving..." He broke off and picked up the thought again with new passion. "He gives me such strength! Just knowing that he's there, depending on me, trusting me ... It's indescribable."

"Yes, I can see that," she said softly, and a great shame washed over her. Had she misjudged this man? Was there anything unsatisfactory in that little boy's life that could not be explained by the absence of his mother? She suddenly wanted to know them both better, to make a sane, sure judgment about Tyler Crawford the man, as well as Tyler Crawford the father. "You've done a good job with him," she said, unwinding her arms and making her tone conciliatory. The effect was not what she might have hoped for. He took her compliment with a bare nod of his head, then stiffened and seemed to draw away, as distant and cool as earlier.

"Thank you again. Now if you'll excuse me, I'm tired."

She bristled. She just couldn't help it. She had reached out, however tentatively, and he had rebuffed her. The old, slow anger resurfaced.

"It *has* been a long day," she pointed out caustically. He smirked.

"Don't worry, you'll be properly compensated. Time and a half for overtime, isn't that standard?"

She could have slapped him. Her fingers coiled into her palms. "I don't want your money!" she snapped at him, and a white fire flared in those electric-blue eyes.

He moved forward, and suddenly she was against the wall, pinned there by her fear of coming into physical contact with him. And at the same time she realized she wanted him to touch her again. She wanted him to want to touch her again. But he didn't. He brought his body close to hers and planted a hand on either side of her head, just above her shoulders, but he didn't touch her. Instead he held her with the commanding strength of his blue, blue gaze.

"Just what do you want?" he demanded of her, his voice low and rough, but she couldn't answer. She didn't know.

What did she want? What did she expect? And why was her heart pounding so, every beat an ache? She had not a single answer. For the first time she didn't know her own mind. Confused and miserable, she turned her face away.

In disgust he pushed back, and she could feel his eyes on her, measuring, judging, finding her somehow lacking. She was insulted; she was crestfallen. She was angry, but she couldn't make herself look at him again. So he left her there, wrestling with her pride and her anger, with her fear and a deeply disturbing and unidentifiable longing, until her old, practiced strength took hold again, allowing her to push it all aside, to fold it up like used linen and pack it away in crackly paper—while she went home alone.

# Chapter Five

It had been easier when he'd skulked. At least then he had merely slipped around on the edge of her consciousness, eerie and slightly threatening, but peripheral. It beat the heck out of having him slam doors every half hour and bark orders like some kind of artistic Napoléon. Now instead of skulking around the edges he stomped right down the middle of her life, and she caught herself biting her tongue so many times a day she could hardly close her mouth for the swelling.

By Friday afternoon she was utterly exhausted—not to mention sore of tongue. As she went about her various chores, she kept telling herself that it was only so many more hours until quitting time and that she would have the whole weekend to rest and recoup. She wouldn't even paint, she promised herself. She was just going to lie around and enjoy her privacy. Then quitting time came, and she drove down the mountain to her bungalow through a series of soft, white flurries, and it hit her that winter, lonely cold winter, was on the doorstep, and suddenly she didn't want to face it alone, passing gray days and black nights in that shabby little room crammed with her belongings. Privacy seemed a kind of prison in the drab light of winter, and she knew she was going to paint throughout the weekend. It wasn't privacy she wanted so much as to be secluded from herself, and work was the only way she knew to achieve that.

It snowed on the mountain while she painted, and she met the plow coming down when she was on her way up that next Monday morning. The world was bright and white and glistening, but somehow she felt desolate. Perhaps it was that she had finally decided: however legitimate her concern, Marilyn was wrong. Tyler Crawford was mercurial and enigmatic and sometimes downright insufferable, but he was a decent father. Royce himself was the proof of that. So now what was her excuse for driving up the side of this mountain? She had always been good at putting things aside, a talent developed early in her life, and she put this new thought aside now. The problem with sublimating reason, though, was that it left a person to operate on raw emotion, and her emotions were already pretty raw where Tyler Crawford was concerned.

The man in question had absented himself, however. He was working again, and Cheyenne couldn't help reflecting, with just a touch of envy, what a luxury it must be to simply walk into a room and shut the door whenever the mood arose. Her own schedule required forcing the muse to appear at her behest, and while she was proud of her discipline she was also aware that real success meant acquiring some leeway in one's hours and method of work.

Due to Tyler's "leeway," Monday was quiet. But Monday night it snowed again, and this time it was nearly noon the next day before Cheyenne could get up the mountainside. She realized then that there would be days when she couldn't get up at all, especially when the icing started late in the season. The snowplows would be busy all the time then, and the tourist industry being what it was it would be necessary for them to concentrate first on keeping the roads open to the ski lodges. It occurred to her that the weather might afford her an excuse to bail out of the job.

"I'm sorry, Tyler," she could hear herself saying, "but I can't expect you to pay me when I can't work, but when I can't work I can't pay my rent, so I'll have to look for a more accessible job." The idea was a kind of safety valve, but it didn't seem to make her feel any better. In fact, the only thing that seemed to make her feel better about anything these days was being around the boy.

Royce had accepted her as easily as if she had been a part of his life from the very beginning. Like "Melly," she was treated more as family than hired help, and it wasn't unusual for him to hang around and "help out," figuratively speaking, of course. That's what he was doing Tuesday evening when Crawford yanked open the door to his studio and glared out at them.

"Royce, do you have to beat that broom handle on the wall?"

The boy looked up at the end of the broom handle as if expecting it to detach itself and whack against the wall of its own accord. "I'm sorry, Daddy," he said in a little voice. "It's just too long, you see."

"What are you doing with it in the first place? I'm not paying *you* to clean." That made Cheyenne dig her nails into her palms around the end of her mop. He turned his glare on her. "Isn't it rather late for this sort of thing?" he demanded, and she swallowed to keep from biting off the end of her tongue.

"Cheyenne was late to work today," the boy put in on her behalf. "It snowed again."

"Well, that's Cheyenne's problem, isn't it?" Tyler remarked sharply, and the boy dropped his head in a pout.

"Does that mean I can't help?" he asked in that small voice. Cheyenne wanted to tread on Tyler Crawford's toe, but she stepped around it and went to the boy.

"You've been a great help," she soothed, cradling the boy's head against the top of her leg, "but the broom handle *is* a bit too long for you, and I think I could finish up more quickly at this point alone."

"We could cut it off," he said hopefully, and Cheyenne sent Tyler a venomous look that said, "Now do you understand?" To his credit he pushed out a deep breath and stepped forward, placing his hand on the boy's shoulder. It felt oddly intimate, standing there with the boy between them, and Cheyenne felt constrained to keep her gaze trained on the top of the boy's head.

"We can cut it off," Tyler said, "but then what would Cheyenne use when you aren't around to help her? I think it's better if we just get you one of your own, one your size. How would that be?"

The boy nodded and turned up his face. A smile of innocent sweetness did the same thing to the corners of his mouth. "That'd be great. Can I have a mop, too?"

Tyler sent a look of doubt to Cheyenne, and she looked up just in time to catch it. He seemed to be asking her opinion, and something light and bright rose up inside her. She found herself holding his gaze, considering, weighing, enjoying the moment as if it were a treat. She started to shrug, her feelings toward the boy so benevolent that she was quite willing to overlook the inconvenience of having him slop around with a mop of his own, but then she thought how easy it would be for him to slip and fall. He didn't consider this play, after all. He considered it work, and it made him feel grown-up and responsible to help out. She couldn't take a chance on having him do that when she wasn't around to supervise. She gave her head an all-but-imperceptible shake, while stroking his at the same time. Tyler considered a moment longer, then went down on his haunches beside the boy.

"I think we'd better leave the mopping to Cheyenne," he said gently. "Besides, sweeping's the hardest part anyway."

"Oh, I really need a good sweeper," she added. The boy beamed.

"Okay!" And he hugged both of them, one arm around his father's neck, the other around Cheyenne's leg. They all laughed, and Tyler stood up with Royce still clinging to his neck.

"You know what? I think we'd better let Cheyenne finish up here while we wash for dinner. Melly will be calling us soon."

The boy reached out and hooked his other arm around Cheyenne's neck. "Will you stay and eat with us?" Her eyes collided with Tyler's, and the moment of easy intimacy fled. She drew away as far as she could without putting off Royce.

"I really can't," she said, "I—I have another engagement." It was a lie, out and out, but what could she say? "Sorry, kid, but I don't think I can sit at the same dinner table with your father without thinking about the one disastrous kiss we shared." That would hardly do, especially as it led to other questions, such as, why couldn't she stop thinking about that time? It had been a mistake and an abject failure to boot. No, no, it really wouldn't do to bring it up again. Unfortunately some things just won't stay put no matter how many times they're tucked away.

Tyler stepped back, carrying his son with him. "We really mustn't impose on Cheyenne," he said, his voice oddly strained. "Her evenings are undoubtedly quite busy already." She shot him a penetrating look, not liking the undertone of his speech. "I'm sure there are people lined up outside her door just begging for her attention," he said, and her mouth dropped open at the implication.

"Actually," she said, the hand without the mop going to her hip, "a frenetic social life has never been one of my ambitions. I do have a few good friends left over from my college days, but most of them are married and busy with lives of their own now. They complain they don't see enough of me, but they're really the ones who are too busy, and their husbands don't really seem to like sharing them with a single girlfriend." She added that last part just so her message would be crystal clear, and unless she misinterpreted a second time, he got it—and he wasn't displeased. His mouth quirked at one end, and the blue of his eyes was soft and shimmering. She addressed herself next to the boy alone, covering her own confusing surge of pleasure. "Thank you for your help and the invitation, but we'll have dinner together again another time. Now you'd better run along and wash up."

The boy jumped down and beat a retreat after giving her a noisy kiss on the cheek. Tyler stayed, his hands flopping around a bit as if at loose ends. Cheyenne quickly turned her back and started dunking her mop in the pail, her heart speeding in her chest. What did he want? Why did he stay? And why had she made it clear to him that there were no other men in her life? *Other?* That stopped her cold.

He laughed then, and the sound washed over her like a gush of warm air. She dunked the mop and pulled it back through the wringer. She felt like smiling, and she was trembling.

"You know," he said lightly as she bent to the work. "I think I prefer the other costume, after all. You put me in mind of a feminist milkmaid in that getup."

She let the mop fall to the floor and turned. "A feminist milkmaid?"

He grinned. "Guess that must make me a chauvinist pig."

"I guess it does," she agreed.

"Well," he said, his voice going all soft, "just goes to show how imperfect some of us are."

Now why had he chosen that particular expression? Was this a lopsided apology of some sort or at least an acknowledgment of past unkindness? Whatever it was it made her feel like smiling.

"No one's perfect," she commented lightly.

"But some are more perfect than others," he rejoined softly, completely turning their earlier exchange around on itself. Her eyes widened, and her head slowly pivoted to one side. Did he truly regret it then, the unkindness of the kiss?

He narrowed his eyes at her and pursed his lips thoughtfully, but it was impossible to tell what he was thinking, and suddenly she wasn't certain she wanted to know. Cheyenne turned around and picked up the mop, feeling his gaze on her back. Impulsively she reached up with one hand and pulled the scarf from her hair, shaking her head to free the flaming tresses. She stuffed the scarf into her hip pocket and started to sluice the floor. Her hair slid over her shoulder and across her face as she pushed the mop. She tossed it away with a sweep of her hand and pulled the mop to her. It was only then that she heard him turn to go and listened to his footsteps down the hall. When she straightened a few moments later and glanced over her shoulder, he was standing at the top of the stairs, that small, pensive smile and the look that went with it still on his face.

Tomorrow, she decided, the scarf would stay home, to-morrow and every day thereafter. With a nod of satisfaction, as if he had read her thoughts, he went down to his dinner.

She dreamed of him that night. It was very strange, for in her dream they were not lovers, not even friends. They were in her dream just as they were in life: she was the maid, he was her employer. They sat together in a room, a place. She didn't recognize it, but that didn't matter. There was a low table between them, and on the table was a single sheet of clean white paper and a single brush, its tip thick with white paint. Her own hands were folded demurely in her lap, while Tyler's gripped his knees. She stared at the paper, then slowly lifted her gaze to Tyler's face. He rocked forward gently and smiled at her, his blue eyes so vivid that all else paled in comparison. A breeze began to blow, warm and pleasant. It touched her face and lifted her hair, so that it floated about her head and shoulders, the color darker and richer than ever before. It seemed to her then that the only colors in the world were the red of her hair and the blue of his eyes and the white of that paper and paint, and she was inexplicably happy.

She said, "Hello," and he said, "Pleased to meet you." He put out his hand as he said it, and as her own hand journeyed up to meet his, her hair seemed to grow and grow until it swirled about them, filling the room, enveloping them in bright, vivid color. As their hands joined, palm to palm, a strand of her hair was caught between them. He laughed, and she laughed with him, and then she woke up, thinking that they had somehow backed up and started over, the happiness of the dream lingering within her.

That feeling of well-being stayed with her through the morning, though the cold had seeped into her little bungalow and she never stopped shuddering all the while she dressed. The cold was indeed ferocious, so much so that her old car was difficult to start. By the time she got underway, she was solidly frozen, but still her mood was light and bright, like the sunshine that seemed to illuminate but not touch the world with its warming rays. It was slow going up the mountain, and she shivered inside her blanket coat, the bright turquoise wool scratching her chin and neck. But soon she saw the house, and a welcoming gladness welled up in her. How strange it was that after only a few weeks this place seemed more home to her than the bungalow where she had lived the past several months. Her mood was so fine that she didn't even scold herself for that thought but allowed herself a special enjoyment of her surroundings as she crunched across the layer of frost crusting the half foot of snow upon the ground.

It was Dusting Day, she reminded herself, but not even today would she cover her hair. She gave Mellon a happy wave as she passed by the kitchen, then prepared for the job at hand, humming as she stowed away her coat, rubbed warmth into her limbs and gathered her materials. She was working in the dining room, gently cleaning the eclectic assortment of pewter and silver and china and Navaho pottery with which Tyler had filled the room. Filled was not the proper word, for though the furnishings were massive and the collection impressive, the space was large and uncluttered. She had just decided that it was one of her favorite rooms when Royce came seeking her for no other reason than to bestow a good-morning hug before hurrying off to beg Melly for a cup of cocoa. She felt warm and happy beyond all reason, and her hum had grown to a gentle song that slipped through her lips as she dusted along the low windowsill. It was not so loud, though, that she did not clearly hear the *thunk* on the table behind her.

She turned, a smile at the ready and half expecting to find Royce with his steaming cup, then she blinked, surprised to see the alabaster gentleman standing there, very much out of his place.

"What is the meaning of this?"

She looked up, surprised and stunned by the tone of his voice.

"Of what?"

"This!" He took the statuette in hand and brandished it. "Alabaster is a delicate material! It requires special care! And now I find it pitted and stained and . . . completely desecrated!" He threw up his hands and stalked in a circle, shaking his head, while Cheyenne just stared, so taken aback that she couldn't quite understand that she was actually being attacked! "This . . . this is just ridiculous! I mean, it's inconceivable that an artist like yourself wouldn't know how to properly care for something like this!"

"But I do," she heard herself meekly say. He stopped and looked, then glared at her.

"You have ruined my statue!" he roared, and the very violence of it brought her around.

"Like hell!" She threw her duster onto the table between them, a symbolic gauntlet of challenge. "I have ruined nothing! Not a single item! I have done excellent work ever since I entered this house, despite your grousing and your moods and high-handed—"

"High-handed, am I?" he interrupted, plunking down the statuette again. "Well, that's just great coming from the haughtiest maid since—"

"*Haughty!*" she shrieked. "How dare you!"

"The point is my—"

"The point is that you're wrong!" she yelled. "Wrong! Wrong! Wrong! I did *not* damage your precious figurine!"

"Then who did?" he insisted.

"I don't know! And I don't care! I only know that I did nothing wrong. I was very, very careful with that thing. I am an artist, as you pointed out, and I am also a skilled maid. I know exactly what I'm doing and exactly what I did to that statuette, and you owe me an apology."

He opened his mouth at that, then carefully closed it again, his chin jutting out at a dogged angle. "Perhaps," he said with surprising calm, "I was rash."

"You certainly were!" Her chest was heaving, and she was somehow surprised by that, especially as she felt perilously close to tears. She looked away, her arms folding about her middle, and he cleared his throat.

"You're quite right, of course. In fact, it occurs to me that you are unusually qualified for... what you do, and, well, Mellon is slowing down quite a lot. I mean, it's painfully obvious, poor Melly. So, just to show you that I have faith in you, from now on you will clean the studio." He nodded with satisfaction, took the alabaster gentleman and left the room before she could believe what she had heard. Then he stuck his head around the corner, smiled and said, "Fridays. Yes, I think Fridays. That's a relatively light day in your schedule, isn't it? So, Friday is Shopping and Studio Day. Very good." And he went off again.

Cheyenne balled her hands into fists and screamed.

She lugged the mop and the pail and the disinfectant and the wood soap and the broom and the lemon oil and the upholstery cleaner and a fat sponge and the vinegar and a squeegee to the top of the house, cursing Tyler Royce Crawford with every step. When she reached the door to the studio, she took a few moments to lean against the wall and rest. When she had caught her breath, she straightened, squared her shoulders and rapped soundly at the door. To her relief and delight a very confident, four-year-old voice piped an invitation to enter.

"Come on in!"

She opened the door and stuck her head inside. He was alone at the easel in the center of the window cove. For a moment her heart stopped as she realized he was in a smock and his tiny fingers were all tipped with paint. He was just placing thumbs and pinkies to canvas when she called out to stop him and, leaving her paraphernalia behind, hurried into the room.

"Royce, what are you doing there?" He looked at her and his face lighted with a smile.

"Hi, Cheyenne! Sometimes I paint better with my fingers than these brushes," he said, continuing his careful, if unorthodox, application of paints to the canvas. Cheyenne hurried forward to assure herself that he had not destroyed one of his father's works. One look told her that he had not. The work in progress was a colorful blend of brush strokes and finger smears. She breathed a sigh of relief.

"Practicing a bit of technique, are we? That's very good, but tell me something, young man, did your father give you permission to dabble in his paints?"

The boy bit his lip. "You mean I should've asked first."

She squelched a smile. "That's exactly what I mean. You have equipment of your own, and this is not it. Somehow I doubt your father would appreciate anyone taking liberties with his things, so don't you think you ought to show a little respect for his belongings and not just help yourself anytime you feel like it?"

"Quite right."

She recognized Tyler's voice and stiffened. The man had a way of simply appearing whenever he chose, and it was wearing thin with her, even if they were in agreement. He walked toward them, and Cheyenne instinctively withdrew.

He glanced at the canvas, rubbed the boy's head and cuffed him gently.

"You're welcome to all I have," he told his son, "but it's good form to ask first. Saves one from making mistakes and taking what is not safe or proper. Nevertheless," he added pointedly, "contrary to popular insinuation, I am neither selfish nor possessive—except perhaps with the people I love." He stroked the boy's head as he said this and smiled indulgently.

"I didn't mean to insinuate that you were any such thing," Cheyenne muttered with a measure of petulance.

He waved a hand dismissively and started removing Royce's smock. "Oh, don't worry about it. I'm used to hearing those sorts of things about myself, and I freely admit that there are exceptions." He shot Cheyenne a glance that sent expectant ripples along her arms. "My wife, for instance." He gave the boy a pat. "Why don't you be a good helper again and bring in the supplies Cheyenne left in the hall?"

"Sure," the boy chirped and skipped off. Cheyenne hugged herself, trying to dispel the chill that had followed the expectation. She didn't have time to ask herself what her response to Tyler was all about and was too wary to do so in any event, but she could not suppress the mixture of curiosity and regret she felt when he continued on the subject of his late wife.

"Leah catered to me, I'm afraid," he said, picking up the soiled brushes to clean them. "She had no serious interests of her own, and that allowed her to focus almost exclusively on me." He picked up a stained cloth and began to rub the paint from the tips of the brushes. "I learned to be very selfish and very happy very quickly." He smiled to himself as he continued to gently rub the brushes in the same direction. "She spoiled me," he went on, telling her much more than she wanted to know. "But eventually she seemed to become a little bored. I had my work, after all, and while she respected that, she really had no interest in art. Then came Royce."

As if on cue, the boy practically fell through the door. The broom and pail clattered to the floor and sent him sprawling, but he was up in a flash, all grins and enthusiasm. Tyler boomed laughter and called out that he should not try to bring in everything at once, while at the same time handing Cheyenne the brushes for her to continue cleaning. He took a spatula from a side table nearby and began to scrape the still-wet paint from the canvas. Cheyenne experienced a moment of uncertainty, torn between helping the boy and seeming to reject what constituted an order from her boss. It was the boy's enthusiasm for his chore that decided her, and she started to work the brushes clean with the oily cloth, hoping Tyler would let the subject of his marriage lapse. No such luck.

"Where was I?" he asked, and Cheyenne's head gave a small, involuntary jerk.

"You, umm, were talking about Royce," she mumbled, still hoping to deflect him. He smiled at the boy over the top of the canvas.

"Actually, I was talking about Royce's mother," he said, and Cheyenne winced, her curiosity now thoroughly quelled. "I was thrilled with my son, of course, but I'll admit to a bit of jealousy. His mother was no longer concerned solely with me, and once having begun to develop a life with interests of her own, she grew a little apart, not that we weren't happy—except for one thing, one person, I should say."

An alarm went off in the back of Cheyenne's mind, and she swallowed, pouring unusual concentration into a task she could perform in her sleep. She didn't want to know, yet she heard herself saying, "A person?"

He wiped the spatula clean on the palette and set the canvas on the floor beneath the table, where several others resided. Then he turned to her, and she felt her skin crawl.

"Leah's sister." The hair stood up on the back of her neck.

"Ro-Royce has an aunt?" She tried to make it sound like an innocent question and failed, at least to her own ears. Tyler lifted both brows and flattened his mouth in grim disgust.

"Technically," he said. "The woman's a pariah, a leech. I wouldn't trust her alone in the same room with my son anymore than I trusted her with my wife."

"But they were sisters," she objected, and wanted to bite her tongue.

"Sisters were never so different," he stated flatly. "Leah was soft and warm and generous." He turned away and folded up the easel with a whack-clack-clack, saying, "Marilyn would take advantage of the dead." He carried the easel to the closet and came back to clean and cap the tubes of paint. "Not even Leah could abide Marilyn for very long, so I didn't have to keep them apart, though that was the way Marilyn saw it. The truth is, I tried to protect Leah from her. My poor Leah was no match for her manipulative, grasping sister."

Cheyenne remembered the two of them in college. Calm, sensitive Leah had been liked by everyone, and Marilyn had held on to her sister's popularity with both fists. Yes, grasping was a fair description. And yet Cheyenne had often felt pity for Marilyn. It had always seemed that Marilyn wanted to be liked but continually sabotaged herself, no matter how hard she tried. Cheyenne was no exception to the rule. She had admired Leah and detested Marilyn,

though she was not really a member of either's set. Still, she
had recognized the misfit in Marilyn and did not envy her
having to cope with her sister's natural, unconscious lik-
ability. In an odd way Marilyn had always made her feel
slightly guilty for disliking her. Was that why she had agreed
to involve herself in this insane plan? And now that she
knew the premise itself was insane, did she have any justification for staying on this job?

"Only that I like to eat," she muttered.

"I beg your pardon?"

Cheyenne forced a smile. "I, uh, said that your wife
sounded very sweet."

"Sweet," he said. "Yes, that was my Leah." He had finished cleaning up after his son and was leaning against the
side table, arms folded. "She was so sweet and generous that
she gave that odious sister of hers a sizable fortune. It was
the only thing we ever truly fought about. They had inher-
ited equally, you see, after the deaths of their parents, and
Leah had been quite sensible and wise with her invest-
ments, while Marilyn spent her way through her share in a
matter of months. You wouldn't believe some of the
schemes that woman cooked up to get money out of my
wife, and when I finally demanded that Leah cut her off, the
shameless gold digger married that doddering old fool,
Bray. I understand she's just about run through his fortune
and is now slowly destroying his gallery." He shook his
head. "Why a vicious, greedy shrew like that should be allowed to live as she pleases when my own darling Leah..."

He broke off, a dark, violent look about him, and Cheyenne shuddered involuntarily. This was a worse mess than
she had ever imagined. If he should ever find out that she
and Marilyn... Like him, she couldn't even finish the
thought that most troubled her. Like him, she didn't have
to. The reality was so ugly it could not be dismissed.

"Well." He pushed away from the table and stood upright, smiling thinly. "We go on. We manage, and that's what I actually came to speak about with you."

She hadn't followed him. Only a little earlier she had wished fervently that he would change the subject, and now that he had she was focused so intently upon her dread that she couldn't make the turn. She just stood there, her arms crossed against her chest, huddled against the chilling prospect of exposure. Yet her facial expression must have conveyed some sort of cognition, for he went on, and indeed, some part of her was aware, for she heard him, and the shock was almost physical.

"I want you to move in with us."

She gaped, gasped, gaped again, and the chill fled instantly. He chuckled, but it seemed like some hideous roar to her, and she huffed an angry reproof.

"That...why... Laugh at me!"

He was smiling wickedly. "It's just...the look on your face."

"You have lost your mind!"

"No, I'm being very sensible. Think about it. Royce adores you. He needs female influence. Mellon can't cope as it is, and she's going to want to help with her son's wedding arrangements. And soon, Cheyenne, you're not going to be able to make that long drive up the mountain every day, not in your old car with the snow and the icing. There's a raise in it for you, of course, and as you wouldn't be paying rent any longer, it would be doubly rewarding. Oh, and did I mention the studio?" He lifted both hands in an expansive gesture. "Ample room for two in here, wouldn't you say? Or, if you prefer, you can set up somewhere else. This is a big house, after all. Of course, the lighting wouldn't be as wonderful anywhere else, but it could be done."

He had been speaking very quickly and with a reassuring degree of enthusiasm, and it all sounded so perfectly reasonable—which made her certain that it was not! And yet... To share a studio with Tyler Crawford! How many serious artists the world over would kill for such an opportunity? And the boy... Hadn't she been in this from the beginning for Royce's sake? Wasn't that what she'd been telling herself? Wasn't that the only real justification for what she had done? And yet...

"How can I?" She hadn't intended to speak. The question was one she meant for herself, but it was Tyler who answered it for her. He reached out and gripped her shoulders.

"Because we need you. Royce needs you, Cheyenne, and Mellon needs you, too." He lifted a hand to her chin and tilted her face up so his blue eyes could plumb hers, and her heart began to speed as it always did when those enthralling eyes dipped into her soul. "I need you, Cheyenne," he finished softly.

She almost agreed then and there. She opened her mouth and almost said, "Oh, yes, Tyler. Of course." But then she thought of Marilyn Stiles Bray and the little smirk of derision she had worn at their last meeting and the dark, angry look that had come over Tyler when he had spoken of her, and she disengaged herself and moved away from him, struggling to reason.

"I don't know, Tyler..." she began. But he hadn't played all his cards yet.

"What could possibly keep you from it? You have your choice of rooms, ample work space, more money, convenience. You give up nothing, because, of course, your friends are welcome here just as you are free to come and go and lead your own life. It goes without saying that you would be doing us a great service, especially Royce, and if you find that you are overburdened, we can get someone in to help out on a part-time basis." He laughed and folded his hands together. "You know, Cheyenne, what I'm doing is trying to hire you as a mother for my son—so that should tell you how highly I value what you have to offer us." He smiled at her. "Say you'll do it. Come on, say you'll make your home here with us, and if it doesn't work out—" he shrugged "—there's always severance pay."

*Yes,* she thought grimly, *there's always that.* Because eventually Tyler would find out about Marilyn, and then he would undoubtedly fire her unless... What if she immediately and completely severed her ties with Marilyn? No one but she and her former classmate knew of their arrangement, and if that arrangement ceased to exist before anyone else could find out about it... It was irrational at best, but nothing about this entire mess had been rational from the very beginning. Why start now? She squared her shoulders and lifted her chin.

"I'll move in tomorrow," she said, and the smile he gave her made her think that she was risking a lot more than just her job, but that was one of those thoughts she could stow neatly into a secret compartment in her mind. And that was where it would stay, she promised herself. After all, this was a good thing she was doing, good for Royce and Tyler and Melly and even herself, at least as far as her art was concerned. Yes, in that way it was an opportunity of a lifetime, and she'd be twice foolish to pass it up.

Wouldn't she?

## Chapter Six

Cheyenne stood before the wicker-framed mirror in her bedroom and brushed her hair, while next door Royce made busy truck sounds. She had chosen the room next to his for just this reason: she loved the idea of having him right there, of hearing his happy chatter and answering his needy calls. Besides, there was the added benefit of being constantly reminded of why she was here, and also, she liked the room. It was smaller than some others available in the house, and Tyler had told her it was built with the connecting door and matching decor to Royce's room so he could have overnight guests. He had hoped to dissuade her with that from taking the smaller room, but then he had conceded that the only time the room had been used was on the rare occasions when Royce had been ill and he, Tyler, had wanted to be near him throughout the night. She had smiled and replied that he'd made her point for her, and he didn't argue anymore, but she noticed he'd frowned as he carried her half-dozen boxes up the stairs.

Only hours had passed since then, and yet she felt oddly settled and secure in her new home. This being Saturday, she had no official duties to perform, and after her few things had been moved in and either stored away for safekeeping or unpacked, she had spent the afternoon with her new charge, romping and playing and planning future activities. The day had been so enjoyable that she hadn't even thought of her confrontation with Marilyn the evening before—until she had started to change her jeans for something pretty to wear to dinner.

Never before in her life had she dressed for dinner when she wasn't going out. Yet, when Mellon had announced that dinner would be served in the dining room in thirty minutes, she had heard herself say that she had better go and change. Then, as calmly and naturally as washing her face, she'd found herself going through her meager wardrobe in search of something suitable. It was then that she'd realized she was looking for something that would please Tyler, and Marilyn's caustic words had come back to her.

"You've fallen completely under his spell, haven't you? Just like Leah, he can make you do anything he wants. Can't you see he's manipulating you?"

Now, standing before the mirror in a petal-pink, acid-washed denim miniskirt and peplum jacket with an elongated back, she replayed her argument with Marilyn.

"He's not the ogre you want to believe he is," she had told her angry cohort. "He's a good father and a good man. I've not seen one shred of evidence to the contrary."

"He's fooled you!" Marilyn had cried at her. "Just like he fooled Leah! She was always nice to me until she married him!"

"He resented you, I admit that, but are you certain you didn't give him reason to?"

That had occasioned an explosion of denials and whining self-pity. She'd endured a frantic rehearsal of all the slights and insults to which Tyler Crawford had subjected his innocent sister-in-law, skewed, no doubt, in the sister-in-law's favor, until she'd had her fill and said so.

"I'm not listening to any more of this. It's past history, Marilyn, and it doesn't sound at all like the man I know."

"That's my point! He's not showing you his real self!"

There had been just a moment of uncertainty for Cheyenne, but then the moment had passed, and she was quite sure. Somehow she had just known. Her heart told her Marilyn was wrong, and for perhaps the first time she had been brave enough to listen to it. She still remembered the flash of vicious irritation that had momentarily contorted Marilyn's otherwise lovely face. It had prepared her for the battle that followed.

They had literally screamed at each other, with Marilyn calling her a traitor and threatening to reveal their connection to Tyler. Cheyenne shuddered inside her acid-washed denim, recalling how she had screwed up her courage and invited Marilyn to do just that, saying she was not ashamed of having wanted to protect the boy. It had been a bluff. She was as sure as Marilyn that Tyler would toss her out in the snow if he became aware of their scheme, but she had let Marilyn believe otherwise and toughed it out, and surprisingly, Marilyn had backed down. Then had come the real shocker.

Marilyn had strolled around that garish desk of hers, red nails trailing along its edge, and stood before the hideous black wall. "Well," she'd said, "at least it hasn't been a total loss. There's still the showing."

Cheyenne's mouth had fallen open. "You can't be serious! You can't expect me to go through with that now."

"And why not?" Marilyn had demanded. "We had a deal, and you owe me, you know. I got you your precious job."

They'd argued the point for a while, and Cheyenne had stubbornly pointed out that the reference Marilyn had arranged had had nothing whatever to do with her gaining employment. Still, it was Marilyn who had brought the position to Cheyenne's attention, and one day that reference just might come in handy, after all, as Cheyenne was forced to admit, secretly, that her job was none too secure. Nevertheless, she was concerned about having to explain to Tyler how she had been offered a showing at the Bray Gallery. Still, she didn't suppose she had much choice, at least not at the moment. She tried arguing that she didn't have enough pieces ready for display, but Marilyn insisted she could be patient.

They'd left it at that, but it was a puzzle to Cheyenne, especially as in the very beginning she'd sensed Marilyn wasn't all that enthusiastic about coming through with her suggested showing. She'd figured the showing was just the carrot at the end of the stick, and since her findings had not gone in Marilyn's favor, she'd assumed the showing was a moot point, and yet there Marilyn was demanding compliance. It was a mystery, but one Cheyenne was inclined to hope would simply go away as time passed. And yet . . .

She shook off the sense of foreboding and did a final turn in front of the mirror. Maybe the miniskirt wasn't such a good idea, after all, but a quick glance at her watch told her it was too late to change again. As if to confirm that, Royce swung open the door and hung on the knob.

"Ready?"

"Hey," she scolded gently. "What happened to knocking first?"

He covered his mouth with his hands. "Oops. Forgot."

"That's all right," she said. "You won't forget next time."

He grinned at her. The smile was designed to charm and it worked. "I like your dress!"

"Well, thank you very much. Now let's see those hands." He offered them up, and she did a close inspection. "Very good. Now shall we go down?"

They opened the door and stepped out into the hall, nearly bowling over Tyler.

"Whoa! I was just coming to get you two." He backed up and did an obvious double take, his eyes traveling up and down her body and up again to her face. "Cheyenne," he said, "you look fantastic."

She thanked him, noting that he had shaved, changed his shirt and put on a soft blue sweater, which made his eyes seem even more brilliant than usual. She had a knot in her stomach and a fluttering in her chest, and she couldn't help feeling that they were celebrating. Everyone was smiling and gay, and Tyler and Royce each took one of her arms and escorted her downstairs, where she found the table set with tapers and fresh flowers.

"Mr. Tyler wanted to make your first dinner special," Mellon explained with more than her usual enthusiasm, at which point Tyler cleared his throat and quickly ushered her into her chair.

She and Tyler took opposite ends of the table from which the expansion leaves had been removed, with Royce on one side facing the window. Cheyenne felt a little awkward about sitting down to table with the family while Mellon played the role of servant, but Mellon herself seemed perfectly satisfied with the arrangement. In fact, she seemed downright happy, which struck Cheyenne as strange indeed, but then she was far too happy herself to question anything this night, especially with Tyler smiling at her in the candlelight.

There was conversation, but Cheyenne would never remember what they had talked about or what they had said. The evening would be forever painted on the canvas of her memory as one of softness and warmth: the muted clink of silver on china, the gentle splash of wine in crystal, the murmurs and hushed laughter of comfortable speech, the swish of starched linen. She was living out a fantasy, and she knew it. To be a part of a real family, a happy, healthy family, had been the unfulfilled dream of her chaotic childhood. Other families, she had been sure, ate quiet, elegant dinners and said nice, polite things to one another, but not hers. Dinnertime had always been an uncertainty in her house, either a silent, sullen affair or a podium for her father's raving criticisms and threats. But Tyler Crawford was not like her father. She knew that now, and it was such joyous knowledge. She loved to hear Royce laugh when his father teased or complimented him, and she loved being a part of this, even if it wasn't real, even if it wouldn't last forever.

They lingered so long over dinner that Cheyenne volunteered to clean up, and Tyler sent Mellon off to her own rooms to relax. To her surprise and deep pleasure, and Royce's glee, Tyler insisted they clean up together. They went trundling off to the kitchen with their arms full of dirty dishes and Cheyenne held her breath until Royce delivered the wineglasses safely to the counter. The dishwasher was already busy with the pots and pans Mellon had loaded into it before retiring, so they decided to do things the old-fashioned way, especially as Royce was quite sure that was the way Mellon did the good china and silver.

Cheyenne put him on a stool and let him arrange the dishes on the countertop in the proper order for cleaning:

crystal first, plates next, followed by serving dishes and flatware. Then she started the water, while Tyler rummaged around in drawers for towels. He came back just as the suds were building into a mountain Royce could blow about for a bit and presented her with a ruffly apron, which he himself slipped over her head and tied at the waist, making a large, neat bow upon which he lavished more time and attention than even the most devoted bow connoisseur would have employed. Cheyenne could feel the heat radiating from his hands in the small of her back, and every little brush of his knuckles had an electric charge in it. She plunged her hands into the hot water in an attempt to still the trembling she felt building inside her, but it didn't help much, especially as he repeatedly reached around her to take a dish from her hand rather than across in front of her.

She was quite sure that he was doing it on purpose, which made it all the more enjoyable and nerve-racking at the same time. Still, it was a good time. Electric, perhaps, and a little breathless, but somehow special, and neither of them noticed when Royce sank down on folded arms and drifted gently off to sleep. Only when they were through and teasing each other about their expertise in the field of dishwashing did they notice the dark little head bowed against the countertop.

Tyler walked over and stroked his son's head, gently rousing him. "Bedtime, my boy-o," he said, taking the child into his arms. The boy protested that he wanted to stay up with Cheyenne, and she came over to tweak his ear and rub his back.

"Hey, I'll be here in the morning. I'm not going anywhere. I have a room right next to yours, remember?"

He reached out and sleepily wrapped a hand in her long, fiery hair. "Will you put me to goodnight?" he mumbled, his arm tightening about his father's neck as if he were afraid to lose one of them. Tyler signaled his approval with a direct look, and she quickly acquiesced, feeling warm and happy and needed.

They went up together much as they had come down, and together she and Tyler undressed the boy and slipped him into his pajamas. He was almost asleep even before the last button was buttoned, but he was awake enough to slip an arm about each of their necks and murmur goodnight. Then his dad laid him back, and Cheyenne lifted the covers over him and folded them beneath his chin. He immediately rolled over onto his side, and Tyler bent to kiss his cheek.

"I love you," the boy murmured, and when Tyler responded in kind, Cheyenne bit her lip, touched almost to the point of tears. She intended to content herself with a stroke for the back of his head, but when she turned to move away, he opened one drowsy eye and smiled and said, "I love you, too, Cheyenne," for which she rewarded him with a fierce hug and a nuzzle at his ear. He was sleeping peacefully when they let themselves out into the hall.

This time Cheyenne didn't have far to go. She was home already, and that was such a wonderfully luxurious feeling. She went to her door and placed her hand on the knob, but before she could turn it Tyler's hand was there, covering hers. She had expected it somehow, and somehow she hadn't known what to expect. She told herself, *nothing that happens tonight is real. It's all a dream, a little family dream. I mustn't believe anything that happens tonight.* Everything was topsy-turvy in her mind, but permeating it all was an intense feeling of contentment, of rightness. He took her hand from the knob and turned her to face him. It seemed very close there in the hallway, and he was standing very near. She was acutely aware that their toes were touching, their shoes anyway, her left foot and his right.

"I'm so glad you are here," he said. "We've needed someone like you."

"Thank you." She was surprised to hear her voice shaking.

"I—I hope you'll be happy here."

"I think I will."

"Oh, I intend to..." He backed off and let go of her hand, shrugging helplessly. Puzzled, she studied his face. To her amazement, she realized he was avoiding her gaze.

"What? You were going to say something."

"Not here." He tossed a glance at his son's door. "This is not the place for it." He pushed a hand through his short hair, adding apologetically, "This is so much more awkward than I imagined." She looked at him, completely baffled. He seemed so *shy* all at once that she felt sorry for him, and something was bothering him.

"Do you want to talk?" she asked.

"Very much."

"We could go into the playroom. It's close by and..."

"Ah, why don't we just go down? I, ah, don't want to risk waking Royce."

"All right."

He flashed her a smile and took her hand again, folding it gently within his own. She allowed him to lead her back down, thinking to herself that she was going to get very trim living in this house with its many stairs. He hurried her a bit, and it struck her that he was oddly eager for a conversation about which he had seemed uncharacteristically shy only moments before. She began to think, as they drew nearer the bottom of the stairs and his grin grew wider, that she had been duped. Then, at the bottom of the stairs, they paused a moment, and she stood looking at the big front door with its intricate panes of leaded glass and the tall windows on

either side of it glowing golden with the light of the out-
door lamps.

"It's cold out," he commented softly, and she thought
instantly of how warm and comfortable and safe it was inside. She had never loved a place before, she realized with a
start, and now she had a place to love, a place to want to be.
She looked around her, drinking in every detail: the plush
carpet, the burled woods and stucco, the light colors, the
understated elegance, the exquisite little pieces of primitive
statuary, some of them tucked into Mojave and Yuma Indian pottery. On the wall next to the door that led into the
living room was a tree branch foiled in gold leaf, and beneath that hung an R. Lee White painting that she adored.
She stood and looked at it now, enthralled by its simplicity
and richness. Tyler gave her hand a tug.

"Come," he said, and she followed into the living room,
puzzled again as he paused and seemed to wait for her reaction, but to what? She had been in this room many times
already. She knew it well and thought it the prettiest, most
exquisite room in the house, all terra-cotta and white with
touches of turquoise and bright yellow couches draped with
colorful Navaho blankets. There were shelves stocked with
an impressive collection of *santos*, carved wooden figures
representing the Saints of the Catholic church, some of them
dating back to the seventeen hundreds. They were vividly
painted, and some of the newer ones had glass eyes and ar-
ticulated limbs. They were a benevolent lot, and one of
them, San José, was quite large and stood sentinel beside the
fireplace, which was constructed of red brick and native
rock, its high, wide hearth running the full length of the wall
between the shelves and the enormous cathedral windows at
the front of the house. The whole room was reflected in
those windows this night, from the large brass fixture that
hung from the peaked ceiling, its lights contained within

twenty or thirty tiny terra-cotta pots, to the inviting crackle of the fire on the grate and the gleam of the flame against the brass ice bucket on the hearth. Ice bucket?

It was suddenly as if everything held its breath, as if the world had gone still with waiting for her to understand, and then she did. Her mouth fell open, and she whirled to face him, resentment flaring up in her.

"Now wait, don't say anything, not yet. Just give me a chance here, all right?" He was speaking quickly, and as he did so he reached to the side and dimmed the overhead lights.

"When did you do this?" she demanded, yanking her hand from his. He caught it again and tugged her forward.

"When you were dressing for dinner. I hope the wine hasn't warmed by now, but never mind. It's a very gentle little vintage that I think you'll like."

"You manipulated me."

"Yes," he admitted, "yes, I did. I tried to think of another way, but..." He shrugged helplessly. It was a compelling gesture, but she set her mind against it. "Sit down. Please." His tone was plaintive, soft, and he indicated the pillows piled before the hearth. Cheyenne sent him a withering glance and sat down on the sofa. He seemed amused by this, but settled for piling the pillows against the sofa, facing the hearth and the cozy fire. She crossed her arms and legs, giving her foot an agitated little kick while he went to pour the wine. He popped the cork with a minimum of effort and time and filled two glasses, which had been placed on the tray with the cooled wine.

"Here we are." He offered the glass, which she measured disdainfully before taking it. "To...life," he said, lifting his glass. She ignored his toast and took a deep breath instead of a drink. She felt angry, at herself for being so easily taken in, at him for taking her in so easily.

"Why did you do this?" she asked, but for answer he merely sipped his wine and turned aside. He made a great show of sitting on the floor next to the sofa, of arranging the pillows at his back.

"Join me and we'll talk," he said, looking over his shoulder at her. He smiled beguilingly. "Come on. Have a heart. I know I'm not very good at this sort of thing, but you certainly aren't helping matters any."

"Not very good?" she snapped. "That little act upstairs was masterful!"

He cocked his head to one side, looking up at her. "Yes, but it doesn't seem to be working very well now, does it? And I'm trying very hard."

He was trying. That much was painfully obvious, and hearing him admit it took some of the resentment away.

"I just don't understand," she said into her glass, and then she felt his hand take hers, and she looked down at him. Blue eyes seemed to engulf her.

"Come sit with me. Please."

The resentment fled. She tried to capture it, to cling to it, but it just wouldn't stay in the same place with that blue, blue gaze. She slipped off the sofa onto the floor, confused and wondering. He held a couple of pillows in place for her with one hand and made certain that they fitted into the small of her back against the sofa as she settled down.

"There now," he said, "that's much better. Have you tasted the wine?"

She shook her head, and he prodded her gently until she lifted the glass to her lips, then he drank his, too. It was very good, sparkling and light with a slight sweetness and a faintly woody taste. She took a second sip, thankful for something to concentrate upon besides the man next to her.

"I don't know enough about you," he said, "to know how your tastes run in wine—or much else—so I simply chose the very best from my cellar. Do you approve?"

"I like it very much," she replied, "but I don't know that I approve."

"And of what do you disapprove, Cheyenne? Of me?"

"I don't like being manipulated."

"I apologize. I simply didn't know how else to get you here."

"And why get me here at all?"

He held his glass by the stem and studied it for a moment before draining its contents and setting it aside. He took her glass from her hand and set it aside, also, careful not to spill it. Then, very deliberately, he put his arm around her and moved close beside her.

"I thought perhaps if I set a stage, a very romantic and cozy stage, that it would go better for me."

Her heart was in her throat, beating a heavy, rapid rhythm.

"I don't understand."

He lifted a hand to her face, skimmed her cheek, lightly cupped her chin.

"I have made some women want me, Cheyenne. Given a chance, I think I could arouse your interest, too."

Her eyes flew up to meet his, her mouth parting in shock. Was this condescension? Teasing? What game was it? She simply didn't understand him.

"Sometimes I think you are mad," she said. His eyes flitted over her face, his mouth suddenly grim. He took his arm from about her and looked into the fire, leaning forward against his drawn-up knee.

"Sometimes I think so, too." He sighed and pushed a hand over his face, asking suddenly, "What is it about me that you can't abide?"

Again she was stunned. "Why, whatever do you mean? You confuse me. You—you run hot and cold. You grab, and then you thrust away. You— Oh, I don't know what I'm saying. I don't know what you want me to say." She put her hands to her cheeks and closed her eyes. "I don't know why you brought me here, why you went to such trouble to set the stage for seduction when before you were...displeased."

"Now I don't understand. When was I ever displeased with you?"

She gaped at him, her face blushing with just the memory of that disastrous kiss, his coldness afterward, how he had turned away and dismissed her. "I-in th-the studio," she stammered.

"What about the studio?"

She couldn't answer him. She couldn't say that he had kissed her and obviously had not liked the experience! Why was he doing this? Did he want to humiliate her?

"You know!" she insisted hotly. "Don't pretend that you've forgotten!"

"Forgotten what!" He pushed up to his feet and stalked away. "This is ridiculous! We're talking circles around each other! When did I ever say that I was displeased with you? Good heavens, I've moved you into my home! I've persuaded you to come and care for my son. I've invited you to make use of my studio. How much more confidence can a man have in a woman? And God knows I haven't made any secret of the fact that I'm attracted to you!"

She gasped, and he stopped, staring at her. Now she got to her feet, pushing up her sleeves as if to do battle. "You certainly have!" she declared, and his face screwed into a mask of frustration.

*"What?"*

"Don't give me that! I was there, remember?"

"Where?"

"In the studio!"

"When?"

"The day you kissed me!"

He threw up his hands. They were practically shouting, and she could tell that he was angry. "And what a mistake that was! Be up front, I told myself. Be honest. You're too mature for these insipid games. Show the woman what you want from her. She'll appreciate the honesty—like a bath in ice water!"

"What?"

He glared at her. "I'm a bit out of practice, but I'm not stupid! All right, so you didn't see stars or hear bells, but that doesn't mean it's hopeless. Or is it?"

She stared at him, postured there before the fire, shoulders pressed back, hands at his hips, one leg bearing slightly more weight than the other. He looked inexplicably vulnerable with his blue eyes flashing defensively and the fire playing behind him.

"You are very hard on a man's ego, Cheyenne Cates," he told her, when she failed to formulate an answer for him. "When a man kisses a woman, he likes to feel that she enjoys it, that she finds it stimulating, not that he's just made warm flesh into cold marble!"

Cold marble? Her ears were roaring, and her throat was dry. "Is that what you thought of me?" she asked. "Well, you might have thought that you had caught me very much off guard. You might have thought that you had stunned me."

He held his gaze level. "I thought of that—later, as I was trying to soothe my wounded ego."

She bit her lip. "My ego didn't exactly escape unmarked, either, you know. You did seem displeased."

Understanding flickered over his face then, softening its crags and shadows and making the corners of his mouth curl. He repeated the lines from Robert Burns that he had quoted that day. "'True it is, she had one failing, had a woman ever less?'" He smiled cryptically. "My wit fails me, it seems, and I do apologize. My meaning was not that you were unattractive but that you did not find me attractive."

She felt oddly lighthearted, strangely unburdened, and at the same moment she thought of Marilyn. The image was distasteful, hateful, and she pushed it away, catching his gaze and acting on impulse. "You set a stage," she said. "For what?"

He stepped forward and took her hands in his, lifting them about his neck. "For this," he said, sliding his hands up her arms and over her shoulders to her face. He stepped closer, and she stepped forward to meet him, letting her fingers splay into his hair and over the back of his neck. His hair was stiff and bristly against her skin. She thought it alive, so very much alive. Or was that her? Was that excitement, that verve, her own?

He bent his head toward her, and she lifted her mouth to his, holding her breath until his lips touched hers lightly, when it all went rushing out and her lids shuttered down over her eyes. He took her mouth with such agonizing slowness, such careful, deliberate detail that she knew he was trying to make this special, hoping to please her, and that more than anything else did make it special and pleasing. Not that he had anything to worry about on that score. Tyler Crawford was all man, and the woman in her had been aware of that fact from the first moment they'd met. Something about him reached out to her, made her feel her femininity acutely. Standing there now with her arms about his neck while he plied her mouth with kisses of such intense concentration made her think that she had needs and desires she hadn't even explored yet and that the time might be coming to explore them. Then he slid his hands down her throat and over her shoulders to her back and closed his arms around her, and the time for thought vanished.

He pulled her hard against him, and his tongue invaded her mouth, filling it with that paradoxical turgidness that is singularly male, while at the same moment his body made hers aware of his desire, his hands cupping her hips and pressing her against him, then leaving off to patrol the plane of her back, pressing her, gliding there, insuring that her body fitted itself most accommodatingly to his. Her body responded in every instance as bidden, thighs mating his, the flat of her belly softening to allow the thrust of his manly protuberance, breasts flattening and swelling against the compacted walls of his chest.

With the gentlest nudging her knees buckled beneath her and allowed him to lower her to the floor, her body cling-ing to him as his strong arms and hands took her weight. Halfway down their mouths parted, and he fastened his to the underside of her jaw, from whence it sent shivers of sharp delight throughout her body before moving down the column of her throat and up again to recapture her mouth. They were down on their sides now, his left arm supporting her neck, his hand pressed just above the small of her back to hold her against him, while the right one roamed over the curve of her hip and along her thigh to the hem of her skirt, which it tugged upward before journeying farther down-ward and coaxing her leg to curl up and around his. When she had done so, he reached down and slipped off her shoe, allowing her to lock her heel into the notch of his knee. That persuasive hand then journeyed back the way it had come, over the ankle and up the calf, around the bend of her knee and along the thigh to the curl of her hip and over the curve to the dip of her waist and upward still to the fullness of her breast.

Deft fingers plunged between them, cupping and manipulating the weight of her breast until lightning streaks of desire flashed throughout her body, culminating, it seemed, in the pit of her belly. Then his fingers invaded farther, and the buttons that held together her jacket obediently slipped their holds. His hand swept away the heavy fabric and found the thin, lacy nylon of her bra and pried it aside so that flesh could meet flesh. She sucked in her breath, shivering as his fingers closed over the tender mound, the hard peak thrusting into his palm as his tongue thrust deeply into her mouth and that fiery need in the pit of her belly turned molten and spread. She clutched at him with her mouth and her arms and her leg, needing to bring him into her, to quench the volcano he had awakened. Then just when her need was greatest, when the pressure of the passion had built into a raging inferno that seemed ready to consume the constraints between them, he broke away.

She watched, momentarily bereft, through a passion-induced daze while he pushed off his shoes and yanked the sweater over his head. He had worked the buttons at his cuffs and was opening the front of his shirt before it came to her what he was doing, how far they had come from that careful, deliberate kiss—and how far they would undoubtedly go if she didn't stop now. And still she waited that extra moment, until the last button had been freed and the shirt had been peeled back to reveal his chest, rock hard and fashioned with ripples and rills that were utterly masculine, before she could bring herself to signal retreat.

"Tyler, wait!" she said, springing up and pulling at her clothes. She saw the intent drain out of him with a morbid kind of relief. "It's too fast. It's..." What? She couldn't think of another blasted word. Fortunately he didn't make her find one.

He pulled up one knee and draped an arm over it in re-signed disgust. "I—I seem to have lost what little sense I had when you came into this house, Cheyenne."

"Neither of us has been very sensible, I'm afraid."

He looked back and gave her a smile, reaching out a hand to caress her cheek. "At least we're in this together." The touch was electric, compelling, and he moved closer, craning his head to brush his mouth across hers. "Are you sure you don't want to give in to raging impulse?"

"I'm sure I shouldn't," she whispered, and he gave a desultory nod.

"Will you think better of our bargain and leave us?" he asked, his gaze holding somewhere near the base of her throat. She swallowed, feeling the heat of that gaze more surely than any flame.

"I— No."

He smiled and brought his entrancing gaze to her face. "Brave Cheyenne."

She felt herself a trembling coward just then, with fulfillment unlike any she'd ever known a mere gesture away and she unable to take it. But then was not discretion the better part of valor? She pulled in a deep breath.

"I'd better go up."

"Yes, you'd better," he agreed lightly, and she began swiftly to button her jacket and retrieve her shoe.

"Will you stay down here?" She was just making conversation, trying to hold the awkwardness at bay. He reached for the glass she had allowed him to set aside earlier, his own being empty.

"Yes," he said, studying its contents. "I think I'll stay right here and get mildly drunk before I go up. It's been a long time since I've done that, though not so long as—" He shut up and drained the glass. She stood up, getting carefully to her feet, being very ladylike about it, while he settled against the sofa, the pillows scattered in disarray, his sweater and his shirt and his shoes where they had fallen.

She stood there next to him for a moment, and finally she said, "I'm sorry, Tyler." He looked up at her and smiled, but there was a sadness in him that made her want to fling herself down into his lap and cover his face with gentle, healing kisses.

"I'm not," he said, "and I don't plan to be, so stop troubling yourself about it and get a good night's sleep. I plan to set you up in the studio tomorrow and put you to work."

"You don't have to do that," she protested faintly, but he was studying the fire, and she thought he might not have heard. "You don't have to concern yourself..."

"Yes, yes, I do," he murmured, and then he gave her a last smile, not quite seeing her, it seemed, and said, "Good night."

"Good night." She went quickly, not trusting herself to stay any longer, aching in some vague, private way she didn't quite understand.

He stopped her just as she passed through the doorway into the entry, calling out, "Cheyenne."

She answered him, "Yes?"

"I meant to tell you—you're the most beautiful woman I've ever known."

She turned back, the thrill of that sweeping over her like physical sensation, but beyond the door defined with firelight lay a temptation she couldn't trust herself to resist, and she gripped the need to be sensible, to be careful, to wait, to see what might come from this. She turned toward the stairs and squared her shoulders, whispering, "Thank you."

## Chapter Seven

Royce got her out of bed on Sunday morning with excited jabberings punctuated by sharp bounces that nearly dumped her on the floor.

" 'Right away,' he said. 'Isn't it grand?' he said. 'Bring her up,' he said. So, come on, Cheyenne! Hurry!' "

None of it made much sense, but she allowed herself to be pulled from beneath the covers, because it seemed safer than being catapulted into thin air. He got her her robe from the chair near the window—her friend Vicky had dubbed it "faded fuzzy with string" because of the cord with which she'd replaced the oft-separated belt—and danced around her until she managed to get her arms into the sleeves and pull it up over her nightshirt. She jammed the wrong feet into the right slippers, didn't bother to switch them and hurried out with him pushing her from behind, her hand knotted up in her belt, her hair an amazing jumble and a secret smile on her lips for the boy's infectious enthusiasm.

Her first morning in her new home. She was surprised to find that she'd slept rather well.

"Where are we going?" she asked him on the stairs. He had a grip on her sleeve and seemed determined not to let go, lest she flee back to the comfort of her bed.

"You'll see."

When they were still going up at the third level, she knew.

"The studio?"

"Uh-huh! Wait'll you see." He was speeding up, but she had to pause to stretch. A kink was developing in her back. He gave her sleeve a tug. "Come on, Cheyenne! He's waiting."

"Your dad?"

"'Course."

Her heart raced, and it wasn't just taking the stairs at a clip. At the top she insisted on taking a breather, despite Royce's impatience, to push the hair out of her face, straighten her robe and secure the belt, and most of all, to exchange her shoes. Royce couldn't wait and burst into the studio announcing in a loud voice, "I got her! She's here!"

Tyler appeared on the landing in jeans and an old sweatshirt with the sleeves cut out. It gave him a rakish, faintly dangerous look, and his face was flushed with pure excitement.

"They're wonderful!" he exclaimed, ushering her forward with an arm about her waist. "Honestly, they're extraordinary. You don't mind that I uncrated them, do you? I was curious, you see, and wanted to keep my promise...."

"What promise?" They were the only words she could get in.

"Why, to move you into the studio today. But really, Cheyenne, I didn't expect this. They're not sublime, you understand, but the potential, oh, my, yes! With whom did you study?'' He swept her through the door with that. "You know your style reminds me of Macaione—suddenly everyone wants Macaione!—except it's a bit more defined and the colors are softer. Have you done landscapes?''

She would have told him yes, except that she hadn't heard the question. Sight had overwhelmed hearing. The studio was transformed. Instead of one canvas easeled in the prow of the great room, there were three, one set at an angle from the other two, with enormous pole lights erected along the walls and trained at varying degrees for optimum light. Gray winter lay outside the massive windows, but an almost vertical shaft of platinum light signaled a bright morning on the rise. It all seemed a part of the change, the extra table on the opposite wall with its tidy rows of paint tubes and little barrels of brushes, a pair of clean palettes hanging from a hook on one corner and her own soiled one lying upon the table as if in an honored place. Far forward and to one side, beneath its own pole lamp was Royce's little easel and a small table, lightly stocked. All else was the same, except that the couch was pulled closer to the fire than before and there was a small table with three chairs around it pushed up next to the wall near the door.

"You can still find your own place, of course," he was saying, "but I'm so excited. It's so much more than I expected. I don't know what I expected really, but talent's always surprising, isn't it? That's part of why it entertains us, why we search for and treasure it. You're very serious, I can tell that, but how do you have time for it? It must be agonizing to—''

She started to laugh from sheer joy, and he stopped blabbing to stare at her, in shock at first, then in understanding.

"You approve then?" He lifted his arms to encompass the room, and she nodded gratefully.

"You like my work." It was a statement rather than a question, and she was thrilled to make it. He laughed, too, then.

"I'm very impressed, and I want to coach you, to advise you. It's terribly vain of me, I know, but will you humor me, Cheyenne?"

She could only clap her hands in response. It was more, so much more than she'd any right to expect. He hurried toward the work place he'd created for her.

"Are you hungry?" he asked. "Mellon will be up soon and starting our breakfast, but if you're hungry now..."

"No," she said, understanding that they were going to work at once. Royce was standing before one of the paintings in his pajamas, eyeing it critically.

"I like this one best," he decided. "But it's...it's too..."

"Pink," Cheyenne supplied, coming up behind him. He beamed her a congratulatory smile, and she wondered why on earth she hadn't seen it before. The light, of course. This magnificent light. She felt Tyler's hands on her shoulders. They were deliciously warm and sent shivers of electricity down her back and arms. She fought the urge to lay her head back against him and dissolve into his arms. That wouldn't do. No, indeed, that wouldn't do, not now, not in front of the boy, not with work to be done. She picked up her stained palette and hooked her left thumb into the hole.

"Green?" Tyler asked, but she shook her head.

"Yellow."

He gave her shoulders an approving squeeze. "Good. Now show me, where?"

Within seconds they were immersed. His attention span strained, the boy slipped away and lay belly down on the floor drawing a very unartistic interstellar battle complete with sound effects on his sketch pad. They hardly noticed, wrapped as they were in quiet conversation, each other and

the work; and yet, a heightened feeling of togetherness
bound them with Royce playing there, cocooned in a kind
of security she herself had never known. Taking up the
brush, she thought to herself that this must surely be what
heaven was like. But then Tyler reached around her to indicate with a sweep of his thumb the path her stroke would
take, and their bodies touched, and she felt a stirring of
promised ecstasy beyond even this. It was only later, after
Tyler had gone down and brought up their breakfast—de-
claring that he would have a dumbwaiter installed within the
week—and they sat talking over eggs and croissants about
the paintings and the series of which they were a part that
she thought of Marilyn. Thereafter, the specter of disaster
hung over all, and her joy was tinged with the desperation
of impermanence.

The feeling of impending disaster stayed with her through
the days that followed, but still the joys were great and
many. Tyler did not speak of that night before the fire in the
living room, and neither did she, though it was with them,
it seemed, every moment they were together, which was
often, so often she hardly had time to do her job. Not that
they were alone much.

Royce was almost always with them, and Mellon was
forever about, and on two occasions Tyler had friends up to
the house for dinner and the most stimulating conversation
Cheyenne had ever heard. She met Eulogio, complete with
braids and symbolic feathers, and like Royce she adored
him, especially as he asked none of the awkward questions
the others found impossible to resist. Indeed, she over-
heard him providing his own answers to the particularly attractive wife of one of Tyler's old college pals. He said that
"our Cheyenne" was many things: housekeeper, nanny,
protégée and "dear friend." The woman allowed that some

friends were dearer than others. Sly Eulogio smiled at that and, catching Tyler's eye across the room, commented, "So they are," before moving off in another direction.

Cheyenne surmised from Eulogio's manner that Tyler had discussed her with him, and she was both thrilled and dismayed by what his words seemed to imply. Thrilled because she lived now with the sure knowledge that she loved Tyler Crawford, dismayed because if Tyler should come to love her, the loss would be beyond bearing when Marilyn revealed their complicity, as one day she surely must.

Still, the specter of Marilyn was easy to ignore on days when the sunlight streamed into the studio and she saw her work taking shape with astounding authority and clarity, so that she felt the muse had come to sit upon her shoulder and direct her hands. It was easy to be happy when Royce hung about her neck and murmured his sleepy I-love-yous or when galloping through the trees on Tyler's old yellow mare, while he broke trail on the copper-colored gelding and Royce trotted along behind on his piebald pony. The snow was never too deep there, and they had to go farther up the mountain to sled. And then came the day Tyler broke out the skis.

She had no way of knowing when he had started to ski again after Leah's death, and she didn't want to ask, but it was obvious that the boy, who would stay behind, had never seen the gear before, and the worried look on Mellon's face when they set out told her that this was not a frequent happening. He never inquired if she could ski, naturally assuming that anyone raised in Santa Fe had been on the slopes less than an hour away, but he was rather grim in his assumption as he measured her feet against what were undoubtedly Leah's boots. To her relief, and perhaps also to his, they found the boots too small and went to rent her another pair.

He seemed more lighthearted once they were in line for the lift, but his mood became markedly more somber when he helped her into her chair. She couldn't see his face on the way up, but it was obvious that he was studying the blue slope he had chosen and she had approved, though she was no stranger to the more difficult black slopes farther up. At the top she disembarked and sidestepped so that he had room to line up beside her. They pushed off and skimmed over to one side, looking down on the graceful slope other skiers were now following.

"It was about there," he said, using his pole to point to a spot about halfway down just beyond a small mogul. "Oddly enough, she didn't take the jump. She went around it. I've wondered since if she had a cramp or...I don't know." He shook his head, and she laid a gloved hand on his arm. He smiled down at her, his goggles pushed up into his spiky hair. "You must be wondering why I'm doing this."

"You don't have to explain anything to me," she said, but he sighed, and his eyes traveled to that fatal spot down below.

"It was all so freakish. She laughed at me up here and said she'd beat me down to the bottom. Then she pushed off, and I gave her a good start, because I was the faster, even though she was indisputably the better skier. I watched her swerve past the mogul, and I thought, 'Aha, I'll take her there.' Then she just tumbled. It was wild. She faltered. She tumbled. Her own ski caught her beneath the chin. Her neck snapped, and just like that it was over."

Cheyenne shuddered, and he put his arm around her, smiling faintly. "How awful for you," she whispered.

"Yes, yes, it was," he admitted. "I never thought I could come to accept it, but somewhere along the line I found that I had. Then one day I looked at my son, and I realized life had become quite satisfying again. That's when I built the house."

"It's a grand house," she said, and he smiled again, cupping her chin.

"So it is."

She thought for a moment that he would kiss her, awkward as that would be on skis, but then the moment passed, and he grinned and let her go and pulled his goggles into place.

"Beat you down!" he challenged, and pushed off. She pushed off right behind him, and when she reached the jump she took it and caught him there. They were past the place and soaring, Tyler pulling ahead with ease. He reached the bottom first and broke off his skis in time to catch her in his arms as she came whizzing up in a spray of snow. He kept her from falling, and they laughed and capered, and she helped him clean the clamps on his boots and snap on his skis again so they could go back up, all the way this time to the black slopes.

They stayed with it until the slopes closed at four o'clock, and then shouldered their way through the crowds to snatch half-full cups of coffee before packing in their skis and heading home. He was quiet on the way back, but once or twice when she caught his eye he grinned and cuffed her gently on the jaw. It was only in the garage, when the door was slowly closing behind them and she was reaching up to take down the skis from the top of the car that he spoke. He said just two words, and as he said them he held out his arms.

"Come here."

She didn't stop to think or to analyze; she just turned and flew into his embrace, finding his mouth before he could seek hers, locking her arms about him, one around his waist, the other thrown over his shoulder. He wrapped his arms about her, plying her mouth hungrily, squeezing her so hard she ached even through the layers of her ski clothes. Presently he broke the kiss and took her face in his hands, staring down into her yellow-brown eyes as if trying to see beyond them to the very heart of her. It was dark inside the garage, the electronically timed overhead light having switched off some seconds before, but the last few moments of daylight filtering through the row of windows in the big door was sufficient to read his expression. She had never seen such tenderness on a man nor such desire, and it came to her that if the surroundings had been more conducive she might well have surrendered to the look in those vivid eyes. As it was, they both knew now was the time, if ever the time should come.

He smiled at her but sadly, regretfully, and his gaze flitted up to the stocking cap pulled down upon her head. He lifted a hand and swept it away. She took it from him timidly, averting her eyes while he fluffed out her hair and spread it across her shoulders.

"You are beautiful," he whispered, and he gently took her face in his hands and kissed her again. There was a brief, playful war of tongues, during which her arms went round his neck and his hands went down her back to her waist. Then his tongue coaxed hers into his mouth, and she began to explore, emboldened first by the tightening of his hands at her waist and then by the velvety feel of his mouth and finally by his arms tightening about her as he opened himself to her probe. It was an exciting moment in which she felt he laid himself bare to her and invited her perusal. He let her take the lead, holding impulse at bay while she took the kiss as deep as she dared. At last, breathless and spent, she slowly pulled back until they parted. He smoothed her hair with his hand.

"You are so lovely," he said.

"Thank you, for that and for today."

"Thank you—for today and every day you are with us."

She shook her head, smiling. "I love it here."

He put his arm around her and turned her toward the door. Together they strolled forward. "I've been thinking," he said, "you need more time to work. Why don't we hire someone to fill your old job? You and Mellon could choose—"

"Tyler." She stopped and looked at him. "If you hire someone else to do my job, I'll have to leave."

"But—"

"I can't stay here except as an employee."

"It's a different job now, Cheyenne. Royce demands so much of your time, and with the painting there is hardly a moment for anything else."

"Royce doesn't demand anything," she stated flatly, "and you know it." He started to speak again, but she hurried on. "All right, he likes having me here, but you are the one who really looks after him, and that's the way it should be. My job is to clean your house and to baby-sit on occasion. If you should take that job from me, I'd have no choice but to leave."

He smiled thinly, not quite meeting her eyes. "If that's the way you want it, Cheyenne." He lifted his gaze then, very pointedly. "You can have it any way you want, you know, any way at all."

*Except completely,* she thought. *What I want is for you to love me completely, totally, so much that it won't matter that I conspired against you, so trustingly that you could forget I ever knew or believed Marilyn.*

The pall had descended again. The great specter had risen, and she told herself that if she had an ounce of courage, she would tell him everything now before it was too late, before she lost all that mattered to her. And yet in many ways it already was too late. She had never loved before. Somehow her distrust of men and the very business of surviving and working had combined to build a barrier between her and the male half of the world. She had resented every intrusion—or very nearly every intrusion—of every male into her life. Until now. Suddenly her whole world consisted of a man and a boy, a very special man, a very special boy. Not even her painting was more important than these two. But someday she must lose them. Someday he would find out, and he would look at her with contempt. His eyes would say, "Betrayer! Liar!" And she would go. How could she bear to leave if they should become more to each other than they were now? No, she could not have what she wanted. She shook her head.

"What I want, Tyler, is for things to stay just as they are," she said, swallowing away a catch in her voice. He looked at her for a long moment, with disbelief at first and then with resignation.

"It's up to you," he said. "It always has been. But you won't mind, will you, if I try to change your mind?"

"I—I'd rather you didn't," she managed, but then he slipped his hand beneath the heavy fall of her hair and gently massaged the knot at the base of her neck. Try as she might, she could not deny the waves of electric desire that radiated through her, and she closed her eyes to keep him from reading her need there—to no effect.

"I don't believe you, my darling," he told her softly. "The choice is yours, but I promise you I won't make it an easy one."

She could only force herself to face him, to square her shoulders and lift her chin, but she couldn't hide the pain and desire clashing in her eyes, and she couldn't stop the trembling in her hand as he took it and led her inside.

* * *

Life was not as carefree as before. Tyler had made his intentions plain, and Cheyenne knew that her only hope to subvert him was to keep her distance. And yet, he made that extremely difficult. He was kind to a fault, generous and patient and caring, and always there was that passion burning in him, smoldering just below the surface of his civility and decorum. He made loving him seem the most natural thing in the world for her. He made touching a part of existence, like breathing and a beating heart.

It was nothing for him to sit beside her when he came into a room and found her there, watching a moment of television, perhaps, with Royce or taking a short breather before returning to work. And, sitting beside her, it was nothing for him to put his arm casually about her shoulders. So she took to leaving a room whenever he entered. But as they passed he just naturally reached out a hand to her, stroking a strand of hair, a cheek, the top of her arm, a shoulder. Every touch burned and branded, and though she steeled herself against them, they burned all the more, tingling with the most exquisite heat and stealing her breath away.

She found no respite from Tyler Crawford, not in her job, for all the things she cleaned and arranged and cared for were his, not in her play with Royce, for he was so like his father she could hardly separate them in her mind at times, not even in her dreams for whenever she slept he came to her, either to love or to accuse. She didn't know which was the greater torture.

Only in her painting could she eventually lose herself to awareness of him. Selfish as it was, she took to locking herself in the studio at night until quite late, occasionally even through the night. It was actually more restful than sleeping, and by Thanksgiving she had finished the two paintings she had brought into the house as works in progress.

Thanksgiving itself was, much like her life in general, something of a paradox. It had been years since Cheyenne had participated in a real family Thanksgiving, and this one was all the more special as Mellon's sons, Decker and Calvin, were included. They were both likable young men who clearly admired Tyler and looked on Royce as a kind of surrogate nephew. Calvin, the younger one, was the more serious of the two, and Cheyenne was not surprised when he left early to visit his fiancée's family, but the elder one stayed to tussle with Royce and gab with his mother. Cheyenne gathered that he was something of a bounder who had not found his niche in life just yet. During the course of conversation he mentioned several different jobs he'd held and expressed, to his mother's chagrin, some dissatisfaction with his current employment, but all in all he seemed a decent sort. If there was one thing about him that disturbed Cheyenne, it was the way he watched her with Tyler.

Whenever Tyler was near her, which was often, Decker Mellon seemed to be watching. He had the good manners not to openly stare, but every time Cheyenne glanced in his direction, it was to find Decker's eyes sliding away. His extreme interest began to make her uncomfortable, and Tyler, too, seemed to notice that they were being studied. He became rather proprietary with her, keeping his arm about her much of the time or taking her hand. At the table he had made a point of serving her first after he'd carved the turkey, and Decker had seemed to assign a special significance to that. She had seen his brows rise speculatively, and from that point on he had paid particular attention to the two of them. She was quite certain that he had reached some unflattering conclusions about the two of them, and it did not help that Tyler seemed bent on reinforcing those erroneous suppositions.

By the time the day ended, she felt as if she had been pulled almost into two pieces. On the one hand, it had been the most special Thanksgiving in her memory. On the other, she was appalled and embarrassed to be thought of as Tyler's live-in mistress. She hoped Mellon did not believe what her son had obviously concluded, but there was simply no way to know for sure without bringing up the subject, and she didn't dare do that. How could she explain Tyler's affectionate behavior to Mellon without explaining the rest of it, as well—if she even could? The whole situation just seemed to get more and more complicated.

Perhaps that was what prompted her to start sketching another pair of paintings immediately after the holiday. This time her subjects were two women on horseback. One was dressed in jeans, western shirt and boots, with curly hair tamed by a cowboy hat and a lariat in hand, forearm balanced on the horn of the saddle. She was a working girl, her competence and skill reflected in her expression. The other was a prim, delicate thing balanced sidesaddle in tons of skirt and buttoned boots, her perky little hat perched atop a mountain of intricately styled hair, a parasol in her hand and abject terror on her determinedly composed face. She was distinctly uncomfortable in her male dominated world, and Cheyenne wondered if she didn't have more in common with her Victorian cousin than her modern counterpart. Perhaps because of her empathy, she started the Victorian first, working through not one but several nights in a row, until exhaustion drove her to the sofa before the fireplace in the studio and dreamless sleep at last.

She woke the next day in her own bed. No, not her bed. Her bed was small and cramped, and as she pushed out her limbs in that first delicious stretch that comes after a good night's rest, she found this bed wide and roomy. She opened her eyes, sleep still blunting the realization, and looked

around her. Everything was shades of gray, from the soft-
est and most delicate pearl to richest charcoal with large
flourishes of hunter green and vivid touches of cerulean
blue. She sat bolt upright in his bed in his room and gasped.

"Dear God!"

Moments later he opened the door to the sitting room and
stepped into it, dressed in jeans and a white T-shirt that
conformed to every contour of his muscled chest. He was
unshaven, and the growth of beard on his chin bristled silver in the morning light. He smiled at her.

"You're up earlier than I expected. It's only nine. You can
sleep in if you like." She only gaped at him. "You won't
mind if I shave? My things are in there."

He pointed to the large bathroom, where blue fixtures
against gray tile and dark green paper were brightened by
large frosted windows set in walls of glass brick. Cheyenne
had thought more than once that the room needed plants,
but she thought nothing of the kind at the moment; she
thought only how she had come to be here of all places
and . . . where were her clothes? That thought must have
registered on her face.

"Mellon took them," he said as she sank lower beneath
the covers, "right after she removed them." He wrestled
with a smile and won a questionable decision. "You should
wear a smock when you paint. As it is, the sofa will have to
be cleaned."

"I, er, apologize. I guess I just wasn't thinking." Anymore, she reflected, than she had been when she'd locked
herself in that room wearing only a bagged-out warm-up
suit. At the moment she was acutely aware of the exqui-
sitely clean feel of his sheets on her bare body. The sensation was positively erotic, especially with him lounging there
in the doorway, his bright eyes feeding on her.

"Has anyone ever told you how beautiful you are in the morning?" he asked silkily. Cheyenne felt heat spreading in specific parts of her body, most noticeably her cheeks. "No one?" he asked, smiling at her lack of reply. "I thought not. That's part of it, isn't it? Part of why you hold me at bay?"

She came within an inch of telling him yes, but then she thought it might be best to simply change the subject. She cleared her throat, struggling to sound normal.

"How... how, um, did I get here?"

He came into the room, sauntering casually as if this were an everyday but sublimely delicious experience. He went to the massive wall unit opposite the bed and opened a drawer at about chest height. He went through its contents, chose something and brought it out, still precisely folded. He turned and walked toward the bed.

"You didn't really think that locked door was keeping me out of my own studio, did you?" He shook out the article he'd taken from the drawer. It was a pale blue pajama top with white piping. "I've no objection to you locking the door, of course, not as long as I have the key to open it." He stood beside the bed, the pajama top over his arm, and looked down at her. "The fact of the matter is that I couldn't sleep, and as the solution I craved was not available to me, I decided to work. When I found the door locked and you did not answer my knock, I let myself in with my key and found you collapsed upon the sofa. You still had the palette in your hand, and I honestly think you got more paint on yourself than the canvas. And if you ever push yourself that hard again I shall lock *you* out of the studio and keep the key until I'm satisfied you've come to your senses. Do you understand me?"

"Yes." She added a nod for good measure, the covers clutched beneath her chin.

"Sit up," he commanded smoothly, taking the pajama top in his hand. It took a moment for her to absorb his meaning and another for her eyes to go wide in reaction.

"No," she said, rather forcefully. Tyler grinned and sat down on the edge of the bed. Cheyenne froze, the covers drawn taut over her body.

"Yes. No. Morning does not seem to be your best time for conversation, but never mind. I'm happy just to look at you." Yet, even as he said that, his hand was reaching toward her, belying his words. He brought it back to the pajama. "This..." His voice was suddenly raspy, and he paused to clear his throat. "This will do until we can get something of your own up here."

He offered the top, and she slipped a hand and a long bare arm out from under the covers to accept it, but then she faced the problem of getting into it while lying down. Feeling a bit foolish, she struggled into a sitting position, awkwardly clutching the covers to her breast. But that, too, presented a problem, as it was physically impossible to hold the covers in place, spread the shirt and get into it at the same time. The slightly amused look on his face told her that he had already thought of this and a moment before had been prepared to assist her. She bit her lip, wondering if she should send him from the room, his room. She swallowed and tried to appear unruffled as she invited his assistance.

"Umm, would you mind?"

He took the shirt from her, graciously disciplining a smile, unbuttoned it and spread it to receive her arms. She slipped in first one and then the other, all too aware of his closeness as his arms encircled her, facilitating her movements, bringing the silk pajama up and over her shoulders. Quite deliberately he pulled it together in the front and secured the three large buttons over the bed covers.

"There now," he said, taking his hands away. "That will do, I think. You rest awhile longer. After I've showered and shaved I'll bring you something of your own, all right?"

She didn't think it was possible for her to rest here in his bed, wearing his pajama top while he showered in the next room, but then it would hardly do for her to go running around the house in his pajamas. She nodded her acquiescence and sank down upon his pillow. He gave her a pat and got up to go shower.

She lay there thinking about how she had come to be in his bed and how foolish she was to have gotten herself in this predicament. She wondered what Mellon thought about it and if the boy knew and why life couldn't be simple and clear-cut. She thought, too, how devoid her life had been of the kind of caring Tyler had lavished on her in these past weeks and what a luxury it would be to let herself love him as she wished to. A host of unbidden thoughts came to her then, little things like how he had looked in his tight T-shirt and how it had felt to fling herself into his arms that day in the garage, about his excitement when he had first seen her work and the blatant manner in which he had declared her silly uniform provocative, how he liked to take her face in his hands when he kissed her and the way he liked her to wear her hair all wild and unfettered.

One thought led to another, it seemed, and dangerous as it was, she found herself dreaming about how it would be to share his bed with him. She thought of how easy it would be to welcome him beneath the covers, to bare her body to his touch. She thought of how she would kiss him, bold and aggressive, how she would touch him to light the same fires in him that his touch lighted in her, how she would make him moan with need and sigh with satisfaction and whisper words of undying love and bottomless passion. And then she thought how bitterly he would regret those words and how shallow would seem his satisfaction when he knew the truth about her.

The sense of loss was unbearably real and gave the lie to her reckless dreams, dreams that could never be. She cursed the day she had walked into Marilyn Bray's gallery, the day that had set her on this path of desire and denial. It would have been better, she told herself, never to have known Tyler Crawford and his disarming son. If she had an ounce of real strength, she told herself, she would get out now before it was too late. She would go back to her shabby little bungalow and her safe, confined little world. If...if only... She put her arm over her eyes and tried not to weep.

# Chapter Eight

What's wrong?"

Cheyenne started and lifted her arm from her face. Somehow she hadn't realized the water had stopped running or heard the door open. Quickly she rubbed away the little droplets of moisture that had accumulated in the corners of her eyes, feigning the lethargy of near sleep. Tyler came briskly into the room wearing only blue jeans and a towel draped around his neck. His jaw was cleanly shaven, his short hair spiky and shiny; he pushed his hands over his head, straightening his hair, his eyes never leaving her. She levered onto her elbows and gave him a small, tentative smile.

"How was your shower?"

He stared at her, frowning. "How about a straight answer? You're crying. What's wrong?"

"Nothing! I am not!" But, of course, she was, and she bit her lip, desperate to avoid the subject. "I'm just tired," she grumbled, "and I want to go down to my own bed."

He gave her a sharp look and walked on bare feet to the corner of the bed. He studied her as he took the ends of the towel and rubbed them over his neck and face. "I don't know who you think you're kidding," he said. "You don't want to go back to your own bed any more than I want you to." She wanted to deny that, but she couldn't. She couldn't even bring herself to meet his eyes. He sighed and whipped the towel from his shoulders, dropping it to the floor. "Cheyenne," he said, coming to sit on the side of the bed, "isn't it time we talked about this?"

She shook her head desultorily. "Nothing to talk about," she declared with a sniff. Her hands struggled with one another atop the bed covers. He took one of them, calming it in his own larger, warmer one.

"Oh? What about the fact that we are wildly attracted to one another?"

"I—I don't think we ought to discuss that."

"Then what about love? Maybe we should talk about that."

"I never s-said that I . . ." She had to swallow a lump in her throat and fortify herself with a deep breath. "Don't flatter yourself that I'm in love with you."

"But I do," he said softly, and her skin rippled with gooseflesh at the velvety sound of his voice. "I flatter myself that you are in love with me, because I can't bear to think otherwise." He leaned over her and lifted a hand to lightly caress her cheek.

"Tyler, please," she whispered, but that simple touch seemed to have enlivened dulled nerve endings. Her whole body was awakening to a fresh need of him. It was a delicious, languorous awakening, heedless of the fears and reasonings of her mind. Her hand turned in his, clasping it, and he lifted it to his lips, his other traveling beyond her ear to slip beneath her head and into the pillow of her hair.

"I want you, Cheyenne, and I know you want me." He bent over her, finding with his mouth the spot beneath the curve of her jaw. Her hand he doubled back and brought to rest between her breasts, his fingers spreading out atop it, seeking the fullness of her feminine contours beneath the covers. Her nipples hardened against the silk of his pajama top, and with that her body won, driving back the forces of her fear and temerity.

"Oh, Tyler," she whispered, curling toward him and turning her face just enough to allow him easy access to her mouth. He took it hungrily, gratefully, passion exploding between them. What happened next happened quickly. He pushed the covers back with one hand while holding her head with the other and grinding his mouth against hers, and then he was beside her, thrusting his knee between hers, the seams of his jeans rough against her bare skin. It required only a shift of his body weight to bring him atop her, then his hand plunged downward beneath her, pressing against the small of her back so that her hips rotated forward and brought their bodies into stunningly intimate contact.

The need that burst inside her was both urgent and desperate. Something said to her, "Now. Right now," and it seemed that the same voice had also spoken to him. He rammed his tongue into her mouth, and she found herself moving against him in a shamelessly wanton manner, clutching him to her with mouth and hands and body. Her fingers slid over his bare back and down into the waistband of his jeans. It was then that he pulled his mouth from hers and stated it very plainly, his face above hers, blue eyes delving into her light brown ones with flickering, rapt intensity.

"I'm going to make love to you."

Her yes lodged in her throat, but no never even made it from her brain to impulse. She left it to him, allowing her silence to speak for her, and he began very tenderly to kiss her as his fingers worked at the buttons he had only moments before secured. *It was inevitable,* she told herself, moving against him. *There's nothing I can do about it now. Why should I even ...*

"*Da-ad!*"

That little voice brought them both to a cold, screeching halt, and with only a wild glance and a muffled oath Tyler was springing out of the bed. When Royce came into the room, his father was opening a drawer, his back to the rumpled bed, where Cheyenne reclined on one elbow, her face crimson. Tyler extracted a clean T-shirt from the drawer and quickly pulled it over his head, his voice wavering only slightly as he greeted his son.

"Morning, scamp. Sleep well?"

But the boy's attention was elsewhere. "Cheyenne!" he cried, only innocent surprise in his tone. "What're you doing here?"

"Cheyenne isn't feeling well," Tyler rushed to explain. "She, er, got sick last night while she was working in the studio, and we, umm, were afraid she couldn't make it down to her room, so I brought her here and gave her my bed. I slept on the, ah, couch in the other room—in case she needed help during the night."

The boy accepted every word of it as gospel, and indeed, it wasn't so far from the truth after all. He put on a most sympathetic face, his little brows pulling together in an unnatural wrinkle, his almost feminine lips pressed into a pouty frown. He came to the bed and laid a hand on Cheyenne's forearm.

"Are you all right now, Cheyenne?"

"Yes, dear. I'm just fine."

"Cheyenne needs a bit more sleep," Tyler added, "then she'll be good as new."

Royce turned a worried face to his father. "Will she be all right for tonight?" he asked hopefully. Tyler laughed and ruffled the boy's hair.

"Yes, she'll be in fine shape by tonight."

Cheyenne looked askance from Tyler to Royce. "What's tonight?"

"I promised Royce we'd put up our tree tonight."

"Tree?"

"The Christmas tree!" Royce crowed helpfully. "Mellon says they've already got decorations up all over town, and Dad ordered this big, big tree and a little one for my room, too, only it's a live one in a big pot, and we're going to plant it along the drive after Santa comes. Isn't that a good idea?"

Cheyenne managed to smile and say that it was, but a great sadness had descended upon her. Christmas. Thanksgiving had been hard enough, being a part of the family and yet not, loving it and knowing it must all end, having Tyler touch her and put his arms around her and worrying what others must think. She wondered if she could bear that kind of bittersweet joy again, and then she realized everyone was waiting for her to say something, and she looked up to find Tyler staring thoughtfully at her over the boy's head.

"I'm sorry." She tried to laugh. "What were you saying?"

Tyler put his hands on Royce's shoulders, his eyes studying her. "Royce is trying to finalize his shopping list. He wonders what you'd like for Christmas."

Tears stung the backs of her eyes, and it took a great force of will to smile, but she managed it for Royce's sake. "Do you know what I really, really need? New slippers."

The boy's face screwed up. "Slippers?"

"Umm-hmm, you know, house shoes."

"Oh, bedroom slippers!"

"That's right."

"Well, I'm not saying whether I'm going to get them or not!" he declared, glancing knowingly at his father. Cheyenne played the game, sticking out her bottom lip in a pout of disappointment.

"Oh, I hope you do," she said, but he only wiggled his eyebrows and folded his arms, as if to say that wild horses couldn't drag this secret from him. Tyler smiled in amusement.

"Listen, pal. Our Cheyenne needs some rest, so you run on now and let me finish dressing so I can get out of here. Okay?"

"Okay. Mellon says breakfast is ready when you are."

Tyler shot Cheyenne a look that clearly indicated his displeasure at further interruption, but he smiled at the boy. "Tell her I'll be down directly." The boy nodded, crawled onto the bed to give Cheyenne a kiss and ran from the room, happy as a lark on the first day of spring.

Tyler gave her a long look, which she did her best to avoid, then went to another drawer and opened it. He came back quickly and sat down on the edge of the bed, pulling on his socks.

"I see by the expression on your face," he said, "that it would be useless to try to pick up where we left off."

She nodded, careful not to meet his gaze. He sighed and stared at the floor.

"And when next I try to make love to you..."

"Don't," she whispered, burying her face in the pillow. "Please don't."

"Sweet heaven, Cheyenne!" he erupted, lunging sideways and flopping her over onto her back. "What's the point in this? Don't you realize that if Royce hadn't come in when he did, we would be making love *now*. Doesn't that tell you something?''

"It tells me I must be out of my mind!" she cried, wrenching away from him to turn her face into the pillow.

"It tells me that you want it as much as I do," he insisted, brushing her hair back. "Why can't you admit that?" She simply shook her head, tears falling onto the pillow.

"Wh-what would it look like? What would Mellon think? What would ev-everyone else think if we...if we..."

He stroked her temple. "Mellon would think I was a very lucky man," he told her gently, "and Royce adores you, you know that. I don't give a fig what anyone else thinks."

"But I d-do," she insisted to his pillow.

"And just who is it that presents the problem?" he asked. "You have no family besides us, Cheyenne, and surely your friends would be glad to see you happy."

"But I wouldn't be happy," she blubbered, "not for long!"

"I happen to think that I could make you happy and keep you that way for a very long time indeed," he argued, but she could only bite her lip and sniff.

"That's because you don't know, you don't understand."

"What?" he asked. "What don't I know?"

Her eyes went wide, and she caught her breath, realizing how much she'd said. She thought, just for an instant, that she ought to go ahead and tell him. He was bound to find out sooner or later anyway. *Why not get it over with now,* she asked herself, *before what nearly happened before finally does happen later?* But when she sat up and looked at him, saw the concern and the frustration and the obvious desire, she panicked. She couldn't do it. He loathed Marilyn Bray, and when he knew that it was because of Marilyn and her sneaky schemes that she, Cheyenne, had even come to be here in his house and in his bed . . . She closed her eyes against that dreadful eventuality and took the coward's way out.

"Y-you don't understand m-my feelings. M-my relationships with m-men have not been very enjoyable. I never learned to . . . trust a man. My father, you know, was abusive and unpredictable, and because of that I didn't even try to date in high school. I just couldn't be sure how he'd react about a boy coming around. Then when I got into college there were the professors who pinched and patted and the students with only one thing on their minds. It just didn't seem worth the effort, and later . . ." She took a deep breath and plunged on, hoping one confession would bring some relief from the guilt of harboring another. "Did you know I lost my last job because I slapped my boss? It was a formal dinner party, and I'm sure he thought I'd just have to stand there and let him grope me under the table. Anyway, I didn't."

He was clearly shocked and appalled. "Who was that jerk?" he demanded, then the fullest implications of her revelation dawned on him, and he reached out to take her in his arms. "Oh, my darling," he said urgently. "You can't believe I'm like that. This isn't anything like that. You must know I would never take advantage of you. Cheyenne." He curled a finger beneath her chin and tilted her head back so that she could see his face. "You must know that I love you, we both love you, Royce and I."

Christmas. It was Christmas come early. It was everything she'd ever wanted and lacked in her life. It was the dearest thing ever said to her. She closed her eyes and laid her cheek against the hollow of his shoulder, basking in the joy of the moment, holding it against disaster like a shield.

"Oh, Tyler," she whispered. "If only . . ."

"What?" he said, nudging her head back again. "If only what?"

"If only you'd give me a little more time," she said, feeling horribly disloyal. He kissed the tip of her nose.

"Of course, it needs time," he said. "I won't press you anymore, I promise, but you mustn't be angry with me if I have difficulty with that. I want so much to be touching you all the time."

She put her arms around him then, unable to resist this little bit of additional folly, and they held each other for a while. Then, very gently, he pushed her back upon the pillow and pulled the covers into place beneath her chin.

"There now," he said, kissing her forehead. "We've made some progress, haven't we?" She nodded happily and snuggled down. "You get some sleep. I promised my son you'd be fit and well for the tree."

"Yes," she said dreamily. "The Christmas tree."

He rubbed his nose against hers. "It goes against my every inclination," he teased, "but I'll bring you some clothes later."

"Just my robe will do. I can make it down to my room in that."

He kissed her and got up to go to the closet for his shoes. He slipped them on standing and went to the door.

"Sleep well," he said, "and dream of me."

"I'm sure I shall," she answered softly, "and Tyler..."

"Yes?"

"Thank you."

He smiled and went out, closing the door behind him. It was a long while before she wept again, realizing anew how very much she stood to lose.

She only pretended to sleep after Tyler left her all alone in his big bed. By noon she couldn't stand it anymore, so she got up and insisted on dressing in jeans and a big sweater and doing something useful. That something useful turned out to be a leisurely trip to town with Mellon and Royce to pick up the new Christmas decorations Tyler had ordered.

It was cold, but the sun was out, and the day was bright. Everyone seemed in a mellow, relaxed mood, and Cheyenne wondered if Tyler had told them to take it easy with her. Coming down off the mountain with Santa Fe laid out before them like a strange, artful mixture of past and present, Mellon remarked that the sun would make slush of the city snow, and Cheyenne, who was driving, promised to take it slow. That marked the speed for the day, slow and leisurely.

They took their time at the little crafts shop where Tyler had ordered the handmade ornaments, watching the artisans blow and twist the glass into incredible shapes, then frost and paint or etch them. Cheyenne bought one for herself to remember the day by and had the engraver carve the date on the bottom. Then she bought one for Mellon, too, and another for Royce, who cradled his as if it were a fragile egg and looked up at her with such adoration that it made her ache with longing.

After stowing the ornaments in the car, they stood in line to have coffee and mint cocoa in the swank new El Cacahuete, or The Peanut, so called because of its tiny size, then strolled along the city sidewalks, dirty with muddied snow, to window-shop until they were thoroughly chilled again.

It was a fun and relaxed time away from the house and the pressures of her unresolved relationship with Tyler, but she was appalled at how quickly she tired, how deeply she had exhausted herself. She noted, however, despite her weariness, that Royce seemed particularly taken with a small, computerized robot going through its preprogrammed paces in the window of a certain department store, and she measured with some surprise the rapt desire on Mellon's face as the older woman stood staring at a display of furs farther down the street.

On the way home in the car, with Mellon driving, Royce stood up in the back seat to lay a hand on her shoulder and ask if there wasn't something she wanted for Christmas. She kissed his little hand and smiled over her shoulder, saying, "I want you not to get hurt, that's what I want. Now sit down and buckle your belt." He obeyed at once but continued to question her until she gave him a short list of small items: a certain novel that had caught her interest, a green scarf, a pair of galoshes, barrettes for her hair. He stored the bits of information away like a squirrel piling up nuts for the winter, and she hugged herself with the knowledge that she was bound to find one or more of those small items under the tree on Christmas morning. She started then to plan her own Christmas shopping list and was still puzzling over what to get Tyler when the first exquisite ornament was hung on the tree.

He had built a roaring fire on the living room hearth, and Mellon had brought in a pot of coffee with small bowls of flaked chocolate and powdered orange peel to add to it, along with a tiny carafe of peppermint schnapps. Eulogio showed up, his young nephew in tow, a quiet, wide-eyed youngster wearing a printed scarf tied around his short hair. Royce was enthralled with him and assigned himself the task of drawing the newcomer into the bosom of the family. The adults left them alone by mutual consent, and soon the two boys were giggling as they hung the majority of the ornaments on the lower section of the huge tree.

Knowing they would have to rearrange the tree later when the boys were away, the adults sat back and let them have their fun, chatting companionably amongst themselves.

Eulogio always spoke softly and earnestly, while his bright eyes, in contrast, seemed forever delving, studying, observing. His frank gaze told her he had not missed the way Tyler's arm draped casually about her shoulders, nor the little hugs and pats and strokes he dispensed unthinkingly whenever she was near. Once Tyler took her cup from her hand and drank from it, and Eulogio looked away as if not wishing to intrude upon their intimacy with each other. Cheyenne was certain that he blushed, and her own cheeks pinked in response. She sensed a certain unease in Eulogio or perhaps a sadness, and it occurred to her that *she* was the intruder. She had made a twosome a threesome, and she wanted to tell this gentle, talented man not to begrudge her this little time; he would not have to share his friend for long.

She was glad when Tyler took his friend aside for a private chat and busied herself with the boys so Eulogio would not think she minded. But then Tyler came back and took her hand in his, saying that it was time to bid Eulogio and his nephew goodbye. They escorted the pair to the door, and Tyler left them long enough to get their coats. Eulogio watched him go, then turned his divining eyes full on Cheyenne's face.

"He is happy," he stated, and the unspoken assumption was that she was not, and therefore, Tyler could not remain so. She smiled lamely and replied as reassuringly as possible.

"He's a very special man."

The dark eyes turned away, and she had the feeling that she had been tested but that the verdict was uncertain. It suddenly seemed terribly important to her that he know she would not willingly hurt Tyler, that she loved him desperately, even, she was willing to admit, selfishly. She seized his forearm with both her hands and found she could not think what to say to those intense black eyes. Then suddenly Tyler was returning with their coats, and she watched in awe as Eulogio's solemn face dressed itself with warmth and friendship. *He really loves him,* she thought, and it occurred to her that no one had ever felt for her the depth of friendship this mysterious man felt for Tyler. She was deeply, profoundly glad and grateful—and for just a moment grievously envious.

Then they were bundling into their coats, and the frigid night air was sighing through the opened door, and Tyler put his arms around her and stroked her in a manner that raised more gooseflesh than it banished, and she knew she would forego any friendship for the kind of love she felt in his touch. Eulogio nodded to her, clasped Tyler's hand, patted Royce's shoulder and ushered his timid nephew into the night. In the warm afterglow of his abiding friendship Tyler hugged them both, she and Royce together, and she could not stop herself from returning his affection, from belonging, from needing.

She was tired, but she went back downstairs with Tyler after they'd put a sleepy Royce into bed and helped him to properly distribute the hand blown ornaments over the tree. It was a tall tree, a Douglas fir, lushly green and thick, and they had to use a stepladder to reach the very top. Tyler had lifted Royce up to place the angel earlier, and Eulogio's nephew had been given the honor of setting her halo with the star suspended above it by a thin, rigid wire. As a result both angel and halo were dangerously askew atop the tree, and Cheyenne went up to straighten them as the last order of business.

Tyler held the ladder for her, and as she stepped down again, she came into his arms. He held her there for a moment, his hands on either rail of the ladder, while she kept herself rigid between them, fighting the pull of her desire.

Then he dipped his head and put his mouth to the delicate underside of her jaw just below her ear. His lips parted, and his tongue slid out to lave heat along the lower curve of her jaw, then his teeth closed ever so gently on the soft flesh drawn tautly beneath her chin, and she melted, literally. Her insides were suddenly warm and wet and swollen, and she wanted desperately to be touched, to be stroked and held and joined, and she remembered that moment in his bed when he had thrust himself between her legs and it had not been enough. Oddly, she longed to feel that again, to have him that close to her and to feel her body clamoring for more.

Tyler seemed to sense what she was feeling. He left her for a moment to dim the overhead lights, leaving only the twinkling colors on the big tree against the black windows and the glow of the fire dancing with its skewed image upon the glass; then he came back to her and led her to the couch.

Standing there, he kissed her, then stopped to push his hands up beneath her sweater, covering her breasts, and watching as she caught her breath and fought with the resulting onslaught of sensation. Then suddenly his hands were skimming over her body to the waistband of her jeans, and she felt the snap give and the zipper part, and a kind of panic seized her. The fear was dual: that he would not stop and that he would. She felt utterly helpless to dictate either one, and yet she said something; she wasn't sure what, but it must have sounded like a protest, for he shushed her and said, "We won't go too far, love, I promise. Not tonight, not until everything is as it should be, not until we both know it's right. Trust me with this. I promise."

As he spoke, his hand slipped down into the open front of her jeans, and she found herself clinging to him, breathless and weak and totally acquiescent. He kissed her, and it was heady and uncontrolled this time, his mouth and tongue demanding and promising in the same instant, hungry and giving, inflaming and inflamed. When he stopped this time, she was definite in what she wanted: more. And she showed him so, clutching him to her with hands and mouth, until he turned his head away and took her hands in his own and, sitting, tugged her down into his lap.

She was much too enthralled to even know what was expected of her, and he had to turn her physically, lifting her legs onto the couch and pushing her arms up around his neck before she understood. This was for her. This was all for her. He was taking nothing in this except the pleasure of giving. Such generosity of love was overwhelming, over-awing, and she began to repay him with small kisses on his neck and ears and long manipulations of his mouth. He let her do as she pleased for a while, then quite firmly took control.

He put his hands up underneath her sweater and fumbled with the hook on her bra until he freed it, kissing her mouth and chin gently as he did so. He slid his hands around to the front and grasped the mounds of her breasts, kneading them until she felt they would explode, so swollen and turgid that the nipples thrust against his palms with more urgency than she'd thought her body capable of feeling. In the pit of her belly a wet fire was licking upward, heating and flooding her with needs she hadn't imagined she possessed.

He pulled cushions up and forced her back against them, so that she lay across his lap, sloe-eyed and trembling and breathing rapidly through her mouth. He lifted the hem of her sweater and pushed her slackened bra out of the way, then bent his head and took her nipple into his mouth, one hand reaching across her to cover the other, while his free hand slipped downward and crept beneath the opened zipper of her jeans.

His fingers curled to fit her, and his mouth traveled from one nipple to the other, his tongue scouting the path so that her own fingers curled against his short hair, urging him onward. Then he began to stroke her, randomly at first, lightly, patiently, waiting out the shudders his caresses sent coursing through her. They seemed to build, those shudders, each more violent than the last, until they were almost painful in intensity, and she felt she couldn't bear them anymore.

She lifted his head then and, craning forward, kissed him on the mouth, her nipple hard and wet and cooling against his palm as his hand came quickly to cover it. Soon he had kneaded it warm again, and it was then that his other hand began to stroke rhythmically, the strokes growing shorter and firmer as his tongue swept the inside of her mouth and plunged into its moist, rosy cavern. Moments later he was no longer stroking but rubbing, and that quickly became frantic as she lifted and moved against him, moaning into his mouth as the ecstasy rolled over her in wave after luscious wave, cresting finally in a swirling, fathomless crash of need and fulfillment. She closed her eyes, seeing lights in the blackness behind them, and hung on to his neck, trembling and dizzy and delightfully sated.

She curled against him, almost weeping with the sheer joy of it, and he held her, kissing her gently on the ear and the cheekbone and the corner of her eye and finally on the mouth again, lingeringly, lovingly. He was trembling, too, and she clutched him tightly, holding him, basking in the warmth of his generosity. They held each other for a long time, watching the fire and the lights winking on the tree they had decorated together with people who cared and mattered. Finally he took her face in his hands and turned it up to catch the flickering light and summed it all up, all the beauty and warmth and joy she was feeling.

He said, "I love you," and she knew it was everything that had ever truly counted in her life—and soon it would end.

## Chapter Nine

The days flew by with preparations for Christmas and, surprisingly, the wedding of Mellon's younger son. Much to everyone's surprise, Calvin's fiancée's recalcitrant father suddenly agreed to allow his daughter to marry before the holiday, and Mellon was thrown into a state of near euphoria and sheer panic.

The wedding was to be in a small Catholic church on the mountainside with the family priest presiding, but at Tyler's insistence, the reception was to be in the Crawford home, courtesy of Tyler Crawford himself. He declared it his present to the newlyweds, and they were only too glad to take him up on his offer. Cheyenne decided, with Tyler's encouragement, to paint portraits of the happy couple, and it was arranged for the two of them to come after the first of the year for formal sittings.

The occasion afforded Cheyenne ample reason to keep busy. She turned the house upside down and inside out, dusting and polishing every nook and cranny, every knob and knot until the whole place gleamed like one huge, ornate Christmas ornament. That served to keep her apart from Tyler a good deal of the time, which seemed to be the only way she could deal with her feelings for him, for when he was near she just naturally found herself reaching out to him, touching, nuzzling, sharing secretive smiles. Apart from him, she would determine to behave herself. Then he would walk into the room or out onto the landing, and she would just automatically go to him, touch his cheek, his shoulder, his hand, smile. Sometimes she would actually hug him before she could think, and he would laugh and hug her back, and she would be so happy. Then, alone, she would think about it and decide she was just adding fuel to the fire and promise herself it wouldn't happen again—then it would. And on and on it went until she realized the only safe place for her was away from Tyler Crawford.

Yet, she could not stay away, and even as she congratulated herself on maintaining fifteen, sixteen, seventeen minutes of separation, she missed him every second of it. When he showed, her heart would leap and she'd forget all about keeping her distance again. Even at night when the opportunities were greatest for "crossing the line," she could not keep herself from him, and it was only due to Tyler's patience and steely control that they did not make love. In her saner moments she thanked God for the promise Tyler had made her the night of the tree, as she'd come to think of it, and the rest of the time she cursed that promise and everything that had caused it to come about.

But it was easy to forget the negative things with Tyler near and a wedding to prepare for and Christmas coming. It was easy to be happy and gay and busy one's self with details and preparations, so that only in the still, alone times did she remember that it was all transitory, temporary. She would weep then with the anticipation of unthinkable loss, and sometimes she found herself praying that what she knew must happen would not, and she would remember with wrenching clarity doing that as a child: anticipating her father's rage and scathing retributions and praying they would not happen. But they always did, and *that* she could not forget, so that even in the happiest, gayest, busiest moments a shadowy, nebulous cloud hung over her. Sometimes she thought she could learn to live with it, but deep down she knew better, even when she was happiest, like the morning they cut the greenery.

No one and nothing escaped Tyler Crawford's artistic penchant, and he had decided that he would bring the forest inside. He was as excited as a kid on a great adventure, and his excitement infected everyone around him.

He hauled Cheyenne and Royce out into the snow and up the mountainside to cut greenery, but not just any greenery. Every bough had to conform to a certain shape and weight and length, and he took great care to brush the snow and ice from each one before the cutting. It took the better part of the morning to select, cut and transport the branches back by piling them on the sled and allowing them to slowly edge their way down the mountain. Add to that the snowball battles and the playful tackles and tussles, the slipping and sliding and laughing, the kissing away of snow and the warming of bodies all zipped up in down-filled coats and the morning became afternoon before they even knew it.

They came stamping into the house, all pink cheeked and runny nosed, famished and deliriously jolly, and Royce related for Mellon the most entertaining moments of their battles and games while Cheyenne and Tyler gobbled down a very late lunch like greedy children. They weren't finished, though, for there was the arranging and the tying of the branches to be done. This Royce could not do, so it was up to Tyler and Cheyenne to deck the mantel and the chandelier in the living room, the banister that descended into the entry and the table in the dining room. They stood greenery in the windows and tucked tufts of it dressed with holly among the baskets and the statuary. They made a glorious wreath for the front door and garnished it with ribbon and brass bells, and just when she thought they'd done with it, Tyler brought out the tiny white lights, yards and yards of them, and they began stringing them through the greenery.

The house smelled and looked like an evergreen heaven, and though her hands and forearms were raw and stinging, Cheyenne felt it was definitely worth it, especially when she stood looking up at the chandelier in the living room, entranced by the lights shining within the graceful boughs above, and Tyler stepped up behind her and put his arms about her and hooked his chin over her shoulder. He was holding her like that when Mrs. Mellon came into the room with a small pot of fragrant orange cinnamon tea. Guiltily Cheyenne's cheeks pinked again, but Mellon only smiled and put her hands together and declared how wonderfully beautiful it all was. She thanked them warmly for all their hard work, and then began to speak about the amaretto wedding cake she was baking and how she would arrange the reception tables between the dining room and the entry, and would it be permissible, did they think, to serve warm spiced apple cider instead of punch? And could she use the Spanish lace tablecloths as well as the Israeli linen?

Tyler said it was all up to her, she should only remember that the mariachi band would be set up on the five broadest steps at the bottom of the staircase. Mellon gasped and clapped her hands and threw her arms out. She hadn't known about the band, and wouldn't everyone be thrilled, and whatever would she wear to the wedding? Tyler laughed and yelled for Royce at the top of his lungs, going out into the entry. Cheyenne and Mellon exchanged curious glances and went out behind him.

"Bring it down!" Tyler was shouting at the boy, waving his arm. "No use waiting for Christmas when there's a wedding!"

He smiled at the women, his mood obviously expansive. A few moments passed before the boy appeared on the second-floor landing. He wagged an enormous box, a flat, rectangular thing of white cardboard that bulged in the middle and trailed a wisp of white tissue paper. Tyler laughed delightedly, hurrying the boy with his own joyful anticipation, so that Royce spilled it at the bottom of the stairs and the coat came tumbling out. Mellon gasped and began to cry, her hands at her cheeks, while Cheyenne could only stare in puzzlement and wonder.

Tyler snatched up the coat and whirled around with it. Young Royce clapped and sang, "I told him! I told him! I seen you looking at it!"

"Saw," Cheyenne automatically corrected, but no one paid her the slightest attention. Mellon was weeping big, fat tears, and Tyler was settling the coat onto her shoulders.

"There!" he announced. "Anything you wear will be perfect under that!"

"Oh, I don't believe it!" Mellon cried, stroking the glossy brown mink. "I never dreamed ... I never expected ... Oh, Mr. Tyler!"

It was pandemonium for a moment, with Mellon dripping tears and hugs everywhere, and Royce still proudly proclaiming that he had been the one to tell. Somewhere in the middle of it all Tyler swept Cheyenne into his arms and kissed her hard and possessively on the mouth, and her body reacted instantly with a moist, warm flooding of desire, and she kissed him back, clingingly, belongingly. Afterward she noticed that Royce's eyes were wider and brighter than usual, and he was smiling to himself as if he'd just finally found out the happy secret everyone else had been carrying around with them. Mellon seemed to take it in stride, or perhaps she was just too overwhelmed with the coat to notice.

"Mr. Tyler, I just can't..." she began, but he hushed her with a quick, engulfing hug.

"Oh, Mellon, I'm so happy!" he said. "We're having a wedding in this house, and it's Christmas, and Cheyenne's here, and we have you to thank for most of it!" For some reason Royce threw his arms around Cheyenne then, and she hoisted him up onto her hip, so overcome by the feeling of family and belonging that she herself was close to tears.

"You're too good, Mr. Tyler," Mellon was saying. "It's so wonderful to see you like this!" Then she, too, turned and hugged Cheyenne, getting her and the boy together. It left her feeling warmly responsible for all the good things going on around her, for the joy and generosity and laughter. It was the happiest moment of her life—and then the telephone rang.

Cheyenne put Royce down to go and answer it, not because she had a premonition about who was calling, but because she was feeling so responsible and maternal and in control. She could hear Mellon gushing thanks over Royce and Tyler in the background when she picked up the receiver of the phone mounted on the wall beneath the staircase and spoke into it, the smugness of satisfaction in her tone.

"Crawford residence. Cheyenne speaking."

"Well, now," said the cold, deliberate voice on the other end, "isn't that a stroke of luck—for you."

She nearly dropped the phone. Marilyn. The dark cloud descended with a thud that she felt most profoundly in her chest. Her immediate reaction was panic, but anger quickly overcame it. How dared she call here? What if Tyler had answered? Heart pounding and thus steeled, she gritted her teeth and replied in a low voice.

"I don't want to speak to you."

"That's just too bad!" Marilyn hissed confidently. "You'll either talk to me, or I'll talk to Tyler. Take your pick."

Cheyenne swallowed and gripped the telephone receiver, panic surging again. "What do you want?"

She felt immediately as if she'd capitulated. *Coward,* she thought, and guilt swamped her the instant her mouth closed on the last word, but it was too late to take them back. It had been too late before she'd said them.

"I want those paintings," Marilyn said. "You promised me the paintings."

"I—I can't. It's out of the question."

"Now you listen to me," Marilyn went on brutally. "I don't care about the showing, not now, not right away, but there's been interest, considerable interest, in the ones I had—"

"*Had?* You don't mean to say you've sold them!" Horror overshadowed any thrill she might have felt, not that she hadn't sold paintings before, though never from a gallery with the clientele and standing of the Bray—and there was the rub. She didn't want anyone to connect her with the Bray Gallery, no one, ever. It was a vain hope, she knew, but she couldn't help harboring it.

"Of course, I sold them!" Marilyn was prattling. "And don't go thinking you've got money coming. You owe me. I got you your job and I've—"

"Yes, yes," Cheyenne interrupted sharply. "I don't care about any of that. I don't care about the money, only I can't give you any more paintings. I can't. He would know. I just can't risk it."

She could literally hear Marilyn's smirk. "He would know, would he? Oh, that does sound desperate. You two must be awfully chummy by now. Has the great man played the romantic for you? He was sickeningly sweet with poor Leah, you know. It made me ill, really, to see him fawning—"

"Stop it! Just stop it!" Cheyenne was aware that her voice had risen and become shrill, but she couldn't help it. She couldn't bear for Marilyn to know or even to guess how dear he'd been, how sweet and giving and utterly charming.

"You little fool!" Marilyn was laughing at her. "Well, if you've gotten yourself involved with him that's your problem, but don't expect me to keep my mouth shut for nothing. He'll throw you out, you know. He hates me, and it's quite mutual. I'm terribly disappointed in you. I thought you'd be safe, what with your obvious hang-ups about men. What'd that father of yours do to you anyway?"

Cheyenne caught her breath. No one, least of all Marilyn Bray, had a right to ask such questions with such callousness. Marilyn couldn't understand, of course. Some people could, perhaps, but not someone as spoiled and greedy as Stucky Stiles alias Marilyn The-Grande-Dame Bray. Only people who had had the kind of education life had handed Cheyenne Cates could understand what living with her father had done to her, and they wouldn't have to ask, not like that, not in some mean, flippant self-centered way.

Suddenly the cloud of fear in which she'd been floundering congealed into a cold, crystalline anger. But just as suddenly her vision of the future was quite clear, too, as if the smarmy dreamworld she'd erected between herself and reality had suddenly vanished. The vision was bitter, exceedingly so, but it settled things for her. She had no hope of living a long and joyous life with Tyler Crawford, because she could not erase her association with the one person in the world he despised. She could not change the circumstances under which she had come into this house. She could not rewrite history with the benefit of hindsight. All she could do was handle it, take control, manage the disaster that she could not prevent and perhaps enjoy the little time left to her. She realized suddenly that she'd been indulging a dream, even while telling herself otherwise: that everything would work out, that Tyler wouldn't really have to know and that she could somehow live with the duplicity. She knew now, positively, that it couldn't be that way. *After the holidays,* she decided flatly, and she felt an enormous sense of relief accompanied by a bitter sadness and the determination that Marilyn Bray was not going to call the shots.

She became very still inside, and to Marilyn she said, "You will stop this, right now. You can't intimidate me, so shut up and listen, and I will tell you how it's to be." She felt calm, mature, strengthened by the cool, controlled sound of her own voice. Marilyn, too, seemed subdued; she was silent, anyway.

"I'll come to you after the holidays," Cheyenne went on unyieldingly. "Do you understand? After the holidays. But don't you call again. Don't you interfere with this household, or I promise you you'll never see another painting of mine. Is that perfectly clear?"

There followed a long pause during which Cheyenne set her mouth and remained implacable.

"January second," Marilyn snapped from the other end of the line. "I'll expect you January second." And she hung up.

Cheyenne let out a long, grim breath and put down the receiver. January second. Her world would come to an abrupt end on January second. She needn't dread the end anymore, because now she knew when it would come. In the meantime she could forget about it, live day to day, moment to moment, absorbing all the joy she could hold, like a sponge taking in water against the moment it would begin to leak away, drop by precious drop, to evaporate in the bleak, arid emptiness that would come afterward. She could live and she could love, richly, gratefully until January second. As if materializing out of her dreams, Tyler appeared, smiling and soft eyed.

"What is it, darling?" he asked, and a thrill shot through her, fresh and sharp. She smiled and took his hand in both of hers.

"Nothing. Nothing to bother with now." She slipped her arms around his waist and turned her face up to his, inviting him to kiss. But he stalled, his fingertips caressing her cheek.

"If there is a problem, darling..." he persisted, but she shook her head, smiling up at him with her eyes. He was not to be put off so easily, though. He knew her, she realized with a pang. He knew her so well.

"Cheyenne," he said, his fingertips skimming over her hair, "you know you can tell me absolutely anything, don't you?"

*And I will,* she thought, *but not now.*

His hand was sliding down her back now and over the curve of her hip. That fire erupted in the pit of her groin, and she welcomed it, so familiar now, so right. He was speaking softly.

"I know there's something. It's been right here between us all along, and the sooner we clear it away the better for both of us, don't you see?"

"No," she said, playing her mouth over his.

He hugged her, stopping the kiss before it developed. "Please, darling."

She lifted her hands to his face, gazing up into his eyes.

"I love you, Tyler," she said. "I've been an awful fool, and there are things you'll have to know, but can't we let it wait for a while? Can't we just enjoy the holidays and each other and Royce and the wedding and—"

He kissed her then, crushing her against him with his hands, manipulating her mouth with such beguiling skill that she felt her knees weakening and that desire in her groin blossoming into urgent, hungry need. She laughed against his mouth, and somehow at the same moment tears started at her eyes.

"No one's ever made me feel this way before," she said, breaking her mouth away. "No one's ever made me this happy. Oh, Tyler, let's just be happy for a while!"

"All right, darling," he whispered, and he tightened his arms about her in a massive hug, kissing her ear and the top of her head and the curve of her jaw before fastening his mouth over hers again and plunging his hands downward to cup her hips and press her lower body against his. They stayed like that a long time, torturing each other in the most delicious ways, until Royce called out to them, and they went to him, arm in arm and smiling.

Cheyenne wore white, high-heeled boots laced up over her ankles and a full, pale blue satin skirt over a longer, white lace underskirt and a pair of stiff net petticoats. Her neat little bolero jacket was of the same sky-blue satin as her skirt, and the short, fitted camisole beneath was of white lace, though not of the same pattern as the underskirt or the gloves she wore buttoned at her wrists or the mantilla fastened over her tumbling red hair with a blue, pearlized comb. Tyler looked at her as she came down the stairs and hurried up to meet her, laughing.

"You'll outshine the bride at her own wedding," he said, and right there, with Mellon and Decker watching from down below, he took her in his arms and kissed her. He helped her with the black wool opera cape she had bought at an antique clothing store, its white satin lining faded to yellow against the pristine white of the lace, and his arm remained about her shoulders even after she'd fastened the embroidered frog at her throat.

Royce came in from the kitchen with a milk mustache on his upper lip and bread crumbs on the front of his navy blue sweater. Cheyenne wiped them away with his father's big, linen handkerchief, and then made the expected comment about how his tan slacks perfectly matched his father's and how adult he looked with his little red bow tie fastened to the collar of his white dress shirt.

Tyler was dressed a bit more formally in a white shirt, a blue tie the very color of his eyes with black and brown flecks in it, a sweater vest that perfectly matched his pants and a black velvet jacket. Mellon, of course, was in her mink, with a wine red pillbox hat perched at a sophisticated angle atop her chin-length white hair. The skirt of a wine-red organza dress hung to the floor beneath the hem of her treasured mink and billowed around the toes of her matching pumps, to which were fastened rhinestone buckles. She clung to the arm of her elder son, who was attired as best man in gray morning dress with cutaway coat and pin-striped slacks. Decker Mellon nodded approvingly at Cheyenne and patted his mother's hand.

"I think Tyler and I are escorting the two most beautiful girls at the ball," he said gallantly.

Tyler tucked Cheyenne's hand into the bend of his elbow and smiled down at her. "Yes, indeed," he said meaningfully, "we're very lucky men," and for once Cheyenne obeyed impulse and kissed him quickly on the mouth.

They went out into the garage, and Tyler held the front
door to the passenger side of the teal blue Mercedes while
first Royce and then Cheyenne slipped inside. Decker helped
his mother into the back seat and slid in beside her, while
Tyler went around and got in behind the wheel. The ride to
the church was slow, for the roads became icier and the
snowbanks deeper as they wound their way up the mountainside, but they reached the little adobe church in plenty
of time and were greeted by a nervous young man in a blue
suit whom Decker identified as a younger brother of the
bride. He opened the doors for the ladies, then hurried
around to take the keys from Tyler and park the car.

The church front was a little shabby, but the interior was
enchanting. The foyer, where they parted company with
Mellon and her son, was covered entirely with a mural that
wrapped around all four walls and included the doors, as
well. The paint was cracked and the colors had faded, but
the stylized figures were most striking. A host of angels took
center stage, flanked on either side by shepherds in monk's
robes and sheep scattered across the rolling hills. The cul-
mination was a host of worshipers on the wall opposite,
clothed in the bright patterns and colors of Mexican and
Indian attire.

The candlelit sanctuary was even more compelling, with
sconces along the walls and banks of tapers at the front.
Fresh greenery had been cut and tied with red velvet bows,
and there were pots of poinsettias everywhere. The plaster
had been freshly whitewashed and the dark, rough beams
had been recently oiled. The black wrought-iron railings had
been repainted and the worn burgundy velvet of the padded prayer benches had been brushed until it was clean and
soft. It was altogether enchanting, and though there was no
organ for music, there were six young boys in white robes

and big red bow ties singing softly from the tiny choir deck overhead.

The wedding itself was glorious. The little church was packed, though no more than seventy-five people could have been present. The voices of the boys' choir rang out clear and innocent, while the bride's father's voice cracked and grew gravelly as he gave his daughter in marriage and the priest's rich monotone seemed to fill every cavity with the musical words of the Latin mass. Mellon wept along with the entire bride's family. The bride herself was beautiful, as all brides are. She was a tiny, delicate woman completely overpowered by yards and yards of satin and lace, her shiny black hair done up high on her head with a headdress of silk flowers and netting. The bridesmaids wore dark green velvet with white sashes, their hair crowned in holly, and carried tall, lit tapers wound with ivy. When the priest at last pronounced the couple husband and wife, the girls blew out their flames and set aside their tapers to help the bride lift her yards of netting so that her proud new husband could kiss her. Tyler put his arm around Cheyenne at that moment and held her close at his side, and Cheyenne wept a little herself. Then the whole church erupted in applause, and the choir broke into a rousing, glorious song in Spanish, and the bride and groom ran down the aisle together, beaming with happiness.

Afterward, Tyler and Royce and Cheyenne drove home together while the bridal party and families posed for pictures. Once there, Tyler and Cheyenne were busy directing the caterers and taking care of all those last minute details that any big party entails, while Royce stationed himself at the front door on the lookout for the wedding guests. They started arriving almost immediately, and Tyler called Cheyenne over to help him greet them all, so that they wound up standing side by side welcoming all these strangers to their home. A half hour after the last guest, the wedding party arrived. The time in between was spent taking coats and filling glasses and giving directions to the various rest rooms pressed into service for the occasion, while the band played strangely melancholy tunes in a soft, mournful way. Then sheer pandemonium broke out with the guests all rushing the bride and groom at once. Tyler and Cheyenne stood back, arm in arm, satisfied and very much a couple.

Later, after food and toasts and the cutting of the wedding cake and much kissing and hugging and crowded dancing, the bride tossed her bouquet quite deliberately to her overweight cousin, who giggled shamelessly and made inquiring glances at all the available men. Cheyenne noticed proudly that Tyler was not included in the survey, and she made sure to keep close to him so that the two or three men eyeing her got the same message about her.

They danced, and they ate, and they drank, and they made small talk with people they didn't know and held hands and stroked each other and were lovers for all to see. Then all of a sudden the time had gone, and everyone was lined up shivering on the lawn to throw rice as the happy couple made a dash for their car, decorated with the traditional shoe polish and cans and streamers. People began to leave then, and Mellon was back in charge, ordering the caterers about as if they were her personal staff, and Cheyenne and Tyler took up posts together at the door once more, shaking hands and accepting the thanks of the strangers that filed out into the cold, tossing coats about their shoulders. When the last guest had gone, Tyler closed the door and put his back to it, sighing. Cheyenne laughed from sheer joy, and then they were coming together with outstretched arms and kissing and holding each other.

After a warm, lovely moment, he tightened his arms around the small of her back and looked down at her and said, "Would you like to be married in that little church?"

The question took her totally unawares, and all she could do at first was blink and close her mouth. Then, very carefully, she put some distance between them and swallowed down the lump that had risen in her throat and answered him as truthfully as she could.

"I haven't really thought about getting married at all."

"Then do," he said, tightening his hold on her again. "Think of getting married to me."

Suddenly the bittersweet glow in which she'd been living evaporated, and the awful reality of what lay ahead came back to her, and she knew she couldn't pretend this one away. She could not think of marriage to Tyler Crawford, and she could not allow him to persuade her that she might. She extricated herself from his embrace and looked down at her hands, which fumbled together.

"Tyler, we'll never be married," she stated flatly, and when she looked up she saw his shock and anger and hurt, and she bit her lip, wishing she'd played the game a little longer.

"You would let that happen?" he demanded, puzzling her, but before she could formulate a reply his temper had erupted, and he was pushing his hands through his hair. "What does it take to get through to you? Haven't you ever trusted anyone? Don't you know what it means to love and to be loved? Good grief, Cheyenne, I'm at my wit's end with you and this damnable secret of yours!"

His voice had risen, and the caterer was staring at them, his hands full of dirty plates stacked atop one another. Cheyenne plucked at the front of his sweater, blinking rapidly.

"Please, Tyler, not here, not now. It's been such a glorious day, let's not ruin it, please."

He sent the caterer an angry glare, and the man turned away. He turned the glare on her, and instantly the tears spilled out of her eyes, and just as suddenly his face went all soft, and he growled at the departing anger and gathered her into his arms again. He pulled her close and kissed the top of her head, grumbling.

"I just wish you'd give us a chance," he said. "Dammit! I'm wild about you. I want so very much to make love to you!"

She turned her face up to him, her fawn-colored eyes most grave. "If that's what you want..." she began, but he instantly pushed away from her, his anger flashing again.

"Oh, that's grand! You'll make this supreme sacrifice, will you? Am I supposed to be pleased by that? Why not go all the way and burn yourself at the stake? That would thrill me obviously!"

"I didn't mean it like that!" she told him, her bottom lip quivering so that she sucked it between her teeth.

He glared at her, then pushed his hands over his spiky hair and chanted to himself, "I am a patient man. I am a patient man."

"And a generous one," she added, reaching for his hand and lifting it to her cheek, "and a gentle one and gifted and loving and I want you, too, so very much!"

He growled through the beginnings of a smile and pulled her back into his arms.

"Here I am," he told her huskily. "All you have to do is take me."

"If it was just that simple..." she began.

"It is!" he insisted squeezing her tight. "Why can't you see that? Holy cow, Cheyenne, I've been in love with the whole world ever since you came into this house."

"The whole world?" she echoed, feeling warm and happy despite herself. "That's an awful lot of love, Tyler. Not even you could manage that."

He compressed his lips and eyes, nuzzling her hair. "Well, okay, we can count out one or two of those terrorists running around in the sand over there and a couple of Nazis still hiding out down south."

"And?" she prodded, the warmth fading a bit, the happiness beginning to tatter around the edges. He made a face.

"So add a certain art critic and the guy who beat me to a pulp back in my college boxing days and—" Did he pause, or was that her imagination? "—my sister-in-law."

Cold reality rushed in, and she buried her face in the hollow of his shoulder, shuddering.

"Hey," he said, digging her chin out and pushing it up with his fingers. His voice was soft with concern, his eyes searching.

"Do you really hate those people?" she asked thickly. He stared at her, the thumb and fingertips of one hand skimming her cheeks.

"I love you, Cheyenne. That's what you have to trust."

"Yes," she answered dully. *No,* said the voice in her head. *It's just not that easy. Maybe if I'd been worthy of his trust that would have worked. Maybe for normal people in normal circumstances, people like the Mellons. Mr. and Mrs. Calvin Mellon,* she thought enviously. There were no Marilyns in their backgrounds, no lies and pretenses, only an overprotective father who wanted to hold on to his little girl.

She put her arms around his waist and hugged him close, selfishly holding on. He rubbed her back and whispered something sweet.

"You'll see," he went on. "We'll give it some time. No rush. You just think about it."

She nodded. Oh, yes, she would think about it. She would do that. She'd think about it, grieve about it, every moment for the longest time and often after that for perhaps the rest of her life. She would think that she had loved him and that for a while he had loved her, too, and how it had been doomed from day one, because she had started with a lie she could never, ever take back, because it was the sole reason for her being there. She would think and think and regret and grieve and hold this time to her like the bright and shining gift that it was. But not now, not while the moment was here and she had him to hold. She would think later. On January second she would think of what had been and what could never be.

## Chapter Ten

The lightheartedness had gone. They still touched and still smiled and still groped one another in the shadows and the secret moments of privacy, but it had changed somehow. Cheyenne could not sustain her illusions any longer, not even for those brief moments when they were together, not even when the passion stirred in her and burned hot enough to make her forget that she shouldn't, wouldn't, couldn't ever give in to it. Tyler sensed it. He must have, she reasoned, for though he touched her as often and was as endearing as before and displayed his desire with every opportunity, he was also solemn at times and brooding and even a little sad, as if he no longer really believed it would come together and grow for them.

Yet they were good times, busy times. Christmas was hurtling toward them and with it the gala New Year's Eve bash, which had become a tradition in the Crawford household even since before Leah's time. It was one of *the* events of the season for Santa Fe society, and yet it was oddly informal. There were no invitations sent out, but somehow everyone seemed to feel invited. Terri, Tyler's abrupt, abrasive agent, called to say that she was bringing a party of five in addition to herself.

"I promised the Comptes ages ago," she said, as imperiously as if she were the hostess, "and, well, Net Rucker is my dearest friend. I couldn't exclude her, now could I? And the Curels, tell Ty he simply must meet the Curels. They've this private collection, truly amazing stuff, and we're going to put a Crawford in it. European, darling. We'll be showing in Paris before long, mark my words."

Tyler laughed when Cheyenne relayed the message to him. "Guess those will be our stay-puts."

"Stay-puts?"

"People tend to come and go, you know. The place simply isn't big enough for everyone at the same time. Heck, Santa Fe isn't big enough for this crowd, so it's the out-of-town newcomers and the old-timers who usually wind up staying put for the whole evening."

"I've got the out-of-town newcomers, but who are the old-timers?" she queried.

"Friends," he said. "Eulogio, Tom Kidder, Arch and Mandy Blunt, a few others."

She had met some of those people and heard about the rest. They were "the gang," solid people who liked each other and Tyler. Kidder was a writer, moderately successful, quiet, a little hard to know. The Blunts were ranchers, wealthy, likable, unpretentious. It occurred to Cheyenne that she would see familiar faces in this crowd, perhaps the Gilberts, her former employers and some of their group. She hoped it wouldn't be a problem, and she was wise enough to discuss it with Tyler.

"So it was old Leo's chops you tenderized, eh? Well, don't you worry about him. He won't be staying long."

That worried her. "Tyler, the last thing I want is a scene at this party."

"No, baby, no scene," he promised. "It'll be taken care of well in advance. Honey, in this town all that's ever required is just a phone call to the right people. We're going to send our message via the grapevine, and I can guarantee it will be received and heeded. No, we'll save the scene for *his* next party, only this time I get to bust him."

She folded her arms. "And what if he sends you a message before then?"

Tyler grinned. "Darling, some people send messages, and some people receive them."

She lifted her brows at that, but upon reflection she had to concede that it was probably true. There was a king on every hill, and in Santa Fe that king was art. The Leo Gilberts of Santa Fe society were there just to soak up the culture that dribbled over the edge of the king's cup, and as such they were relegated to a lower strata, while her love, she realized, enjoyed a place right near the top. She took a perverse kind of pride in that, even while disdaining the system that made it so, perhaps because she herself had no real place in it.

Tyler brought in another band, an orchestra this time, and they had to build a special platform for them as the stairs would not accommodate chairs and music stands. There were a trio of caterers this time, one for the canapés, one for the cold plates and another for the beverages. Yet there was no formal bartender, no stable of waiters, only a couple of women to keep things picked up and help with the cleaning afterward. Even the conventional provision of party plates was foregone.

"Napkins and glasses," Mellon stated flatly. "Crates of them."

The preparations were hectic, yet firmly under control. In truth, Mellon did not seem nearly as daunted by providing food, drink and entertainment for the whole of Santa Fe society as she had for her son's wedding reception. But that, too, seemed somehow correct, and Cheyenne developed a kind of laissez-faire about the whole thing, concentrating instead on the family Christmas that was to be hers.

She helped Tyler play Santa Claus for Royce and was given charge of the list. Together she and Tyler crossed off those items they felt were inappropriate or too extravagant, then they scoured the stores for the rest, complaining companionably about manufacturers who spend more on advertising than distribution, thereby creating exorbitant demands for their products and fixing them with exorbitant prices. When that was done, there was her own personal shopping to do.

She had a grand time deciding what to buy for Mellon and Royce and the few others she routinely gave gifts, but nothing she mulled over seemed quite right for Tyler, and at the last minute she was forced to settle for a belt buckle carved from a bar of silver and inlaid with turquoise baguettes. It was a good piece, not the most expensive, surely, but a good find which she felt Tyler would appreciate.

She had to buy an outfit for the New Year's party, too, something gala, but that didn't prove as difficult as it might have. She found it in one of those little out-of-the-way shops where they have everything from carvings to painted plates to garments on consignment. It was silver lamé with a full tea-length skirt spreading out from a dropped-waist bodice brocaded in a lacy design of flowers and twining vines. It had a simple rounded neckline and heavily padded shoulders that overhung to become sleeve caps, and it was utterly backless from the top of the shoulders to the flat of her spine, three, maybe four inches below the waist, where the skirt joined beneath a big, wide bow.

She took one look at herself in the mirror, bought the dress and called Vicky to beg her to do her hair. She hadn't spent much time or thought on Vicky since first meeting Tyler Crawford, not entirely by default. There was too much to explain, and being her only close friend, Vicky always felt entitled to ask the most probing questions. But she managed to convince her to both do her hair and keep the questions to herself—for a while anyway. And even at that she had to bribe her with an invitation to the party and an expensive silk scarf as a Christmas present.

Christmas itself was wonderful, a private, simple, cozy affair. Tyler liked to have the "tree" on Christmas Eve, which meant the family gathered around in the evening to dispense their presents to one another from under the tree, leaving Christmas morning to the sole dominion of Santa, while the afternoon was given to a well-laid buffet and snuggling in front of the fireplace, allowing Mellon the day with her own family.

Tyler seemed pleased with the belt buckle, inordinately so, as his present to her turned out to be a lavish Charles Loloma set of pendant, bracelet and ring crafted from gold, turquoise and coral. She protested at first, but his joy in giving was so evident and powerful that she felt compelled to keep the pieces and treasure them.

Royce took her gift of a teddy bear in a Santa suit to bed with him. They let him stay up late and burn off some of his excitement, then sat before the fire together, holding in their passion by a kind of silent, mutual consent, as if the night were too special, the time too short for dangerous indulgences. After a long while they tiptoed to their secret hiding places and extracted the packages that comprised Santa's delivery, arranging them artfully beneath the tree and whispering about which would be the first to capture his attention and which would hold it the longest.

Then he took her upstairs to her bedroom, and there against the door loosed some of that passion they were holding so tightly. He pressed his body to hers and roamed it with his hands, delving her mouth with his tongue and lips, until they reached that place where either good sense or folly must prevail. And he sent her to bed, tired and heavy with desire, to dream of making love to him, her naked body adorned with only the exquisite jewelry he had given her.

Christmas morning was all it should have been. Royce woke her, too early, by jumping on her bed, and together they went up to drag out Tyler. He fell out in pajama bottoms and grabbed a robe, and they all went down to rouse Mellon in their nightclothes. Royce was so excited he was hopping up and down like a kangaroo, and when they gave him the go-ahead he ran for the living room like an olympic hopeful. By the time they got there he was already tearing into the loot, and it was sheer joy to watch him rip through ribbon and paper and cardboard, exclaim over the treasure revealed, then put it aside to go after the next.

Once the bounty was uncovered and acknowledged, the real mom-and-pop stuff started. They spent hours putting everything together and getting it all in working order. The robot was a big hit, even if it would take weeks to figure out the programming, and there was the buffet to lay out, and as it seemed ridiculous to eat dinner in pajamas everyone trouped upstairs to dress, except Mellon, who had already managed to do so and went off to enjoy dinner at her new daughter-in-law's table. Then suddenly the day was over and Cheyenne found that she was truly exhausted but sated with precious memories, which she would call up later and enjoy at her sad leisure.

* * *

Christmas itself seemed to have come and gone in the blinking of an eye, but the week that followed seemed not to have happened at all. It was as if she went to bed on Christmas Eve and woke on New Year's Eve with a faint, warm recollection of a dream of Christmas morning. *Two days.* The thought came unbidden, clear, sharp and painful. She thrust it aside with the bed covers. Tonight was hers. Today.

She threw on a bathrobe and went out into the hall and along the landing to the stairs, then up a flight and to the left to the den, where she settled into an armchair and reached for the phone. She woke Vicky, listened to her grumbles as she tried to mask the mounting excitement in her voice and set a time for her to come to the house. Then, for just a moment, she looked around her, seeing this room for perhaps the last time. But no, she wasn't going to think like that. Tonight was hers.

She spent half the morning with Royce, giggling over waffles and syrup and storing up the adoration that shone out of his eyes. She was surprised at how calm and upbeat she could be and how deeply she ached inside. It was almost a relief when he went away to do his little-boy things and left her to herself. Tyler and Mellon were busy with caterers and deliveries and the telephone, and when she went to offer her help he kissed her absently and told her all was under control and not to trouble herself. He had engaged a sitter for Royce, a teenage girl with whom he'd had good results before. She would come early and spend the evening with Royce in his rooms on the second level.

"Won't he come down at all?" Cheyenne asked, and Tyler smiled at her.

"If he wants, but he won't. *You* might even want to stay in your room."

"No, I want to be with you tonight."

"I hoped you'd say that." There was nothing absent or mechanical about his kiss this time, and she let it warm and fill her in a way nothing else could.

The remainder of the morning she spent lolling in the tub or wrapped in her robe, reading. Somehow, the inaction made her feel as if she had all the time in the world, as if the hours were not spinning away from her, and then it was time for Vicky to come, and she dressed in sweats and went down to meet her.

They spent a few minutes with Tyler, who was sweet and congenial but obviously preoccupied. He had the good sense and gallantry to comment that neither of them needed special preparation to outshine all the other women who would be there that evening, but his eyes held Cheyenne's when he said it, and Vicky, who was long of body and short of limb and wore her light brown hair shorn in a punky kind of wedge that fell over one eye, laughed aloud and was not fooled into thinking that he actually meant her.

After he left them, the two of them closeted themselves in Cheyenne's little room and wrangled and giggled and finally hit upon a truly attractive arrangement of twists and knots and cloudy curls that played up her bare back and yet accentuated the sheer volume of her hair if not its length. She worried about it a little, knowing that Tyler preferred her hair down, but when the hour arrived and he came to escort her down, the look on his face was enough to tell her that the hair and the dress together were perfection.

He stood there, literally with his mouth open, and stared. Then he took one step into the room, seized her in both hands and kissed her soundly, as if to assure himself that she was real.

"Am I singed?" Vicky quipped after he released her, primping her eyelashes in the mirror, and they all laughed, precisely because the temperature in the room did seem to have risen considerably.

They had to squeeze through the orchestra setting up at the bottom of the staircase, and the looks they received told Cheyenne what a stunning couple they made, she with her flaming hair and silver dress, he with his silvery hair and ink-black tuxedo. They stood, not beside the front door, but in the doorway to the living room, for there were already guests milling about, helping themselves to food and drink. "The earlies," Tyler called them, without the slightest trace of rancor or irritation. Someone brought them drinks, one of the guests, though no one bothered to mention a name. She soon discovered why.

It was pointless, hopeless really, to try to get to know anyone. It was like a carnival, where whole parties blew in, laughing and talking and dancing, perhaps to toast their host, usually in his absence, before blowing out again, only to be replaced by another or even two new groups, some of them with dozens of members. Some only put in an appearance. Others stayed for hours, keeping a steady stream of headlights coming and going on the mountainside and filling up the front yard and even the road so that nothing came or went beyond the house. It soon became obvious to Cheyenne that for the latecomers the trip up was of major significance, and she heard different persons calling out to each other how much time they'd spent just trying to get there, as if the measure of the evening was made in minutes of transportation.

Meanwhile, she and Tyler were having a party of their own, surrounded by their personal friends. The furniture had been moved out to make more room, and there was nothing to do but stand, but no one seemed to mind. The better pieces of sculpture had been moved out, and the Christmas tree had come down, and the place had the feel of a rented hall, but that did not diminish the closeness of the tightly knit group.

They were good people, close but not closed, and they accepted Cheyenne completely because she was with Tyler, and Vicky because she was with Cheyenne. Tom Kidder was even good enough to pay attention to Vicky, who'd managed to turn herself out pretty well in a slinky black halter top and skirt and was having the time of her life just watching the ebb and flow of the tide of bodies.

Cheyenne danced with the men in their group, except Eulogio, who didn't take the floor with anyone, and accepted their compliments with pleasure as they were innocent and sincere and seemed always prefaced by statements about what a lucky slob Tyler was and how well and content he was looking. Arch Blunt even once added Leah to his praise saying, "Tyler hasn't been this vital and enraptured since Leah died. You're a real treasure, Cheyenne, if you can do this to him." She told herself that was something of which she could be proud, that was something good she could leave him out of this, and it helped to assuage a bit the guilt that she felt.

It was hard, really, to converse at any length, even in their small group, for there were constant interruptions: people stopping by to thank Tyler and look her over up close, a little consultation with one of the caterers or the orchestra director. Then there was Terri and her group. The woman was big and horsey and crude in her manner, but she worked the room shamelessly, showing off her European collector and dropping names all over the place. She evidently represented a number of excellent artists, among them a couple of writers, which she pointed out more than once to Tom Kidder, who sipped his drink and maintained a look of disinterest. She came to Tyler repeatedly, making introductions that were instantly forgotten, asking advice she neither needed nor wanted except as a means of demonstrating her stature with her host. Tyler tolerated her, nothing more, and when she had at last overstepped, he put her off with a sharp, direct refusal, which sufficiently cowed her to keep her at some distance for a goodly length of time.

The hours wound down toward midnight, and as the magic moment drew near, the place became more and more crowded, until Tyler and his own party were packed in tight in a corner of the living room. Everything was gay and hectic. People were shouting to be heard above everyone else. Champagne bottles appeared and were passed through the crowd. Some genuine revelers had brought their own funny hats and began donning them. Tyler himself, though weary, seemed jovial and expectant. He stayed quite near her, and as the moments dwindled away, he stood with his arms about her, his chest to her back, taking occasional sips from her glass and nuzzling her ear in a way that let her know he wished they were alone.

Then, suddenly, someone began to count, and soon the whole packed, tipsy crowd was shouting away the seconds at the tops of their lungs. Ten—nine—eight—seven—six—five—four—three—two... By the time they got to one, Tyler had turned her in his arms and had crushed her against him, his mouth firmly planted against hers, his tongue delving deeply. Everything about it said, "This is mine. Take note world. She is mine." A shout went up. The band burst into a rousing rendition of "Auld Lang Syne," and she heard none of it. She heard only that silent declaration of possession.

He held that kiss until people began to pound him on the back and literally pulled them apart with jokes and jostling and best wishes. She found she'd spilled her drink on the carpet, but it was useless to try to do anything about it, and in any event Tyler wasn't letting her out of his grasp long enough to search for a towel and cleaner, even if she could've fought her way through the crowd.

People began thinning out pretty quickly then, though it was obvious some had come to stay until they were thrown out, and still others were drifting in, sometimes for the second or third time. Their own group began to break up with much cheek kissing and hand squeezing, until only Tom Kidder, providing the illusion of an escort for Vicky, and steady Eulogio, with his quiet companionship, remained.

Cheyenne herself was tired, and she leaned against Tyler, welcoming his arms about her, wishing both that the night would end and that it would go on and on ad infinitum, so that her last day, the day of reckoning, would never come. In that sweet, exhaustive time she almost convinced herself that it would not, that God would intervene and stop the moments from ticking away, and then suddenly, in a twinkling, it was all gone. The time had vanished too soon. She had been cheated.

It was Eulogio who alerted her. She felt beside her a looming presence, stiff, protective, inexplicably hostile, and then she heard her name, the voice familiar, smug, cruel in a slick, furtive way. The warmth fled Cheyenne's body. Her heart stopped dead. She could no longer feel Tyler's arms about her or the press of the crowd.

She heard Eulogio saying something in that deep, rumbling voice, heard Marilyn's brittle laughter in reply and then nothing, as if the whole room, Tyler, waited for her to speak. Numbly she forced her eyes to scan the faces about her until she focused on Marilyn's.

She was drunk, or very nearly so, her unnaturally black hair piled stiffly atop her head, red-tipped fingers clutching the stem of a champagne glass with lipstick marks around the rim. There was an older man at her elbow, an anxious look on his square, lined face. He wore a gray overcoat with a velvet collar and carried Marilyn's blue fox over one arm.

"Darling," Marilyn purred, rocking slightly on her stiletto heels. "Let me introduce you to an old friend." The man attempted a smile. Cheyenne held herself regally rigid and looked at him. He seemed terrified. "An old friend," Marilyn repeated. "An old, unworthy friend." She waved her glass, sloshing champagne. "And her—*employer*. Serves you right." This last seemed directed at Tyler, who turned away, sullen, angry, bitter.

"Get her out of here," he ordered over his shoulder, and tossed down a drink he'd gotten somewhere. Marilyn's escort laid a pleading hand on her elbow, but she jerked away, her face turning ugly.

"Tomorrow," she spat at Cheyenne. "And Cinderella turns back into the pumpkin. Happy New Year, chum." She strode away with a sharp, ripping sound, her steps too long for the straight white velvet skirt that flapped about her ankles, now torn to expose a length of tanned thigh above the side split. Her date hurried after her, her coat held aloft in both hands.

Cheyenne turned instantly to Tyler, no explanation, no hope. He sent her a scathing look, his anger cloaking him.

"Chum," he said cryptically. "God, Cheyenne." Just that and nothing more before he pushed his way forward through the crowd. She felt her shoulders begin to shake, then Eulogio's big hands bracing her. She wheeled around, her eyes brimming.

"You knew," she said, seeing it suddenly. He shook his head sadly.

"I know nothing. I only bought some paintings a friend asked me to acquire."

She closed her eyes. "Tyler?"

"He said he couldn't ask you where you'd placed them because you would know he was the buyer."

She lifted her hands to her forehead, blinking away tears. "You didn't tell him who had them?" It was as much statement as question, the answer obvious.

"He is my friend" came the simple answer. "And he loves you."

"Does he?" she asked. "Will he?"

He took a deep breath, searching for words. Finally he shrugged. "Tyler is a man who must love," he said, "his son, his friends, his work, a woman. He was too long without a woman to love. If nothing else, you have moved him that way again. I think he must walk that path."

She thanked him for that, but they both knew he could not say Tyler would walk that path with her.

She did not stay long in bed. There was no point, as she could not find rest there, let alone sleep. Sometime not long after daylight she got up and slipped into Royce's room to stand silently by his bed and watch his innocent slumber. How would she say goodbye? she wondered. What could she explain? She went back to her room, pulled on jeans and a sweater and jogging shoes, then brought out a suitcase and filled it with the contents of her dresser. It was all the packing she could do without going down for boxes, but she hadn't the heart for that. She had made a start, and that was enough for now. First things first. She put on her down coat and went out.

It was not difficult to find Marilyn's house. The phone book gave the address, a prominent one. She was there in little more than half an hour, for the streets were empty and dry, the sanding crews having been out until the wee hours trying to prevent disaster for determined revelers.

It seemed she knocked at the door longer than it had taken her to drive down the mountain and across the sleepy town, and she was surprised when Marilyn herself opened the door, clothed in a filmy pink negligee with too many flounces and ribbons.

"Damn," she said, moving away from the door with a hand to her head. "Couldn't you beg for mercy at a decent hour?"

Cheyenne glanced around the gaudy entry. Black-and-white tile, gold gilt, an enormous, framed mirror with cupids embracing at the top. When she looked back, Marilyn had disappeared through a door at the left. Cheyenne followed, entered the dark, stuffy room to see Marilyn slugging back a drink.

"Hair of the dog," she muttered, wiping her mouth with the back of her hand before pouring another. Again Cheyenne took in her surroundings. The room was in a state of flux. There were bookcases but a notable absence of books. Sofas, of the same style but different coverings, were pushed back against walls that had been plastered but not painted. Shutters covered the windows, some of them just propped there, while bolts of heavy brocaded fabric obviously meant for drapes were stacked on the floor. It looked as if the place were in the midst of redecorating; yet it seemed abandoned, uncared for. Cheyenne turned her attention away. Marilyn was waiting, smug, vindictive.

"I didn't come to beg for mercy," she told her. "I came to tell you there will be no more paintings. Period."

The rage was sudden, blinding. Marilyn threw the glass in her hand. It crashed against the edge of a shelf and showered them with slivers.

"I'll ruin you!" she screamed. "No one in this town will ever give you another showing!"

"I doubt that."

"He'll throw you out."

"I'm leaving anyway."

Marilyn glared at her, her brows and lashes too pale for the disheveled heap of black on her head. "You owe me!"

"Nothing," Cheyenne said. "I owe you nothing. You used me, or tried to. You must have known it couldn't work. You must have known I'd see he isn't what you claimed."

"He's worse!" Marilyn screamed. "I thought you'd see. I thought you, of all people, would be safe from that diabolical charm. You hate men! You think the worst of them all!"

"Wrong," Cheyenne replied softly. "Wrong, wrong, wrong. Maybe once, but no more, and I've you to thank for that."

"He'll cut your heart out," Marilyn uttered, but Cheyenne faced her down.

"It was worth it," she said, and turned to leave.

Marilyn followed her, shrieking. "You owe me! He owes me! He took a fortune from me!"

"He took nothing from you," Cheyenne rebutted, her hand on the doorknob. "Don't delude yourself."

"She left him everything!" she cried. "Our parents' fortune. Leah left every dime to him."

"Not Tyler," Cheyenne scoffed. "She left it to her son, and it was none of yours. It was her share. You blew yours, threw it away and probably your husband's, too, and when sweet, generous Leah didn't cough up her share, you blamed Tyler."

"I need that money!" Marilyn screamed. "What does a boy need with all that money?"

"And you'd have taken it from him, wouldn't you, Marilyn? If you could have convinced me to make a case against that good and decent man, if you could have perverted my mistrust."

"He'll know everything," she promised coldly, drawing herself up. "How you lied, how you schemed, how you betrayed me when you thought you could win it for yourself!"

Cheyenne smiled thinly. "Yes, I thought you'd say that, but it doesn't matter anymore. It just doesn't matter."

She walked out, feeling light and brave and clean, deaf to the filth pouring out into the morning after her.

The house was quiet when she returned, the kitchen cold, the great entry hall silent and forbidding. Cheyenne took some empty boxes from the storage closet and padded lightly upstairs to her room. Working quickly, she began to pack away her personal belongings: pictures, cologne bottles, her little music box. Suddenly the door opened, and Mellon stood gaping in her bathrobe and slippers, a net pinned to her white hair.

"There you are! Good Lord, what are you doing? He came running down barefoot looking for you. You'd better go, quick, before he calls out the police."

"Oh, he wouldn't . . ."

"He would," she insisted. "He said so. He said if you weren't back in ten minutes, he'd report you."

"For what?" she wanted to know, but Mellon didn't answer. She simply stood, wringing her hands.

"Oh, Cheyenne! Whatever have you done? He was crying. I've only ever seen him cry once before!"

Cheyenne gulped and grabbed Mellon's hands to quiet her. "Royce?" she asked quietly, her voice shaking. Mellon sniffed.

"Sleeping."

"Good. You go and fix some coffee. I'll tell you when to bring it up."

Mellon nodded gratefully, as if glad for something useful to do, and squeezed Cheyenne's hands.

"It'll be all right," she said, sounding hopeful, then she went away.

Cheyenne waited several moments, steeling herself and giving Mellon time to make the stairs, then she took a very deep breath and went out. The house was eerily quiet. Down below the floor was littered and scuffed, the carpet soiled. Fingerprints filmed the windows and walls. Confetti hung from the chandeliers, and the sour smell of alcohol clouded the air. Someone would have to clean all that, she thought morosely as she climbed the stairs, someone else.

She didn't knock at Tyler's door. She just opened it and walked inside, through the sitting room into the bedchamber. He was standing before the window, shirtless in navy blue cords and black socks, his hands clasped together behind him. She spoke his name softly, and his head snapped around. His eyes were bloodshot and red rimmed. It was obvious he had slept little, and she suspected he had come up very late, much later than she had.

He looked away, and she followed his gaze to the bed. The telephone was sitting on the fold of the covers he had thrown off when it rang. Marilyn must've dialed the number before her car had even pulled out of the drive.

"Why?" he asked, and she sighed.

"Why did I take this job? Why did I believe Marilyn's lies? Why did I move in here, let myself fall—"

"Why didn't you tell me?" he interrupted hotly. "Why didn't you just tell me?"

"When?" she countered. "When would have been the time to tell? When you hired me? But then I'd never have gotten the job, would I? When I realized Marilyn was wrong about you? There was no point then, and I had nothing else to go to. I hadn't done any harm; you seemed to need me here. So when should I have told you? When I moved in? After? When I knew I loved you? What was the right time, Tyler? I missed it. I couldn't find it. All I could do was just let it run out."

He pushed his hands through his hair and paced back and forth. She could see the thoughts whirling around in his head, but where they were leading she couldn't guess, and that was surprising, because she'd always believed she knew what he'd think, say, do. He stopped and looked at her, brows drawn in, mouth grim.

"What now?" he asked, and she stared at him, puzzled.

"I—I don't know. I'll go."

"Where?" he shot at her. "Where will you go?"

She blinked, stunned. Her mouth fell open. "I haven't thought about it," she told him truthfully. "I haven't thought of anything except you."

He took a deep breath. "Tell me now," he said, "what you were doing for Marilyn."

She spilled it out, how she'd been summoned to the gallery, the deal she'd been offered, the reference Marilyn had gotten for her, the accusations against him and how she was supposed to prove them for some cockeyed custody battle.

"I was the perfect person for what she had in mind, and she knew how to hook me: parental neglect, an innocent child, a job in the house of one of the great modern painters. She missed one thing, though. She thought I'd be immune to you, that I hated men rather than simply mistrusted them. She couldn't know that any woman in her right mind would fall for you, because she isn't, you see. She's warped, terribly warped, and I'm so ashamed that I let her use me."

He was staring at her, his face closed in on itself, crumpled, stiff. She couldn't bear to look at him any longer, and she lifted her hands to cover her face, fighting tears. There was a rustling sound, a quick, hushed swishing that said he'd moved about the room. She wiped her eyes, struggling to maintain composure, and he said, quite abruptly, "Come to bed."

She dropped her hands and gaped at him disbelievingly. He was sitting on the edge of the bed, peeling off his socks.

*"What?"*

He swiveled around and put his feet up, hands linked behind his head. His face had softened, smoothed. She saw his pulse beating at his temple, the remaining lines, the liquid blue eyes. What was that? Anxiety? Relief? What? She shook her head, mouth ajar, and he sat up suddenly, one leg curling beneath the other.

"Do you love me?" he asked, and the breath rushed out of her in one great gasp.

"Yes!"

"And if you were me . . . If it was the other way around, what would you do? What would you think?"

She knew suddenly what he was saying, what point he was making, and it was right. Oh, yes, it was right, and it was reasonable and wise and . . . She rushed toward the bed.

"She's nothing!" she cried. "That silly, warped woman. She's nothing! And you, you're everything. Everything!"

He opened his arms to her, and she partly leaped, partly fell into them.

"Did you think I would let you go? Did you really think I would let you go?"

She kissed him, hugged him, rubbed, grasped. "I love you! I love you! Oh, how I love you!"

He rolled her over onto her back, pushing his hands up her sides, his mouth hovering over hers.

"Marry me," he said, "right here, right now. Just the two of us. And tomorrow I'll take you into town, and we'll see judges, get licenses. I don't know. We'll make it legal somehow."

"And what about that little church up the mountain?" she whispered, her body heating as his hands pushed up beneath her sweater. He laughed softly, nipping at her ear, and great, hot waves washed over her.

"I forgot," he said, "I'm not Catholic."

She pressed her head back and laughed joyously, a wonderful, delicious fire spreading inside her. He kissed her, but she couldn't stop smiling, couldn't stop telling herself this was real, forever, the happy ending she'd dared not hope for.

Ending? No. That was the beauty of it, the great wonder of it. Then it hit her. He'd take her to town tomorrow, after the holiday, and somehow they'd finalize, seal the promises and vows they would make here today. It was fitting, right. January second, her anniversary day, not the end but the beginning of a lifetime of love with this incredible man, who even now was making silent promises she had no doubt would be kept. They were promises from his heart, his wise, discerning, loving, forgiving heart, and she vowed to meet them, beat to beat, thrill to thrill, measure to measure until time itself ceased for them and even beyond with the legacy they would leave: the canvases they would transform, the care they would shower on his son, their brilliant son, the love with which they would fill this house until it spilled out into the city below.

She had known she could learn from him. She had known he could teach her. She had just never dreamed he would teach her to love.

\*      \*      \*      \*      \*

# Silhouette Desire®

## CHILDREN OF DESTINY

*A trilogy by Ann Major*

Three power-packed tales of irresistible passion and undeniable fate created by Ann Major to wrap your heart in a legacy of love.

### PASSION'S CHILD — September

Years ago, Nick Browning nearly destroyed Amy's life, but now that the child of his passion—the child of her heart—was in danger, Nick was the only one she could trust....

### DESTINY'S CHILD — October

Cattle baron Jeb Jackson thought he owned everything and everyone on his ranch, but fiery Megan MacKay's destiny was to prove him wrong!

### NIGHT CHILD — November

When little Julia Jackson was kidnapped, young Kirk MacKay blamed himself. Twenty years later, he found her...and discovered that love could shine through even the darkest of nights.

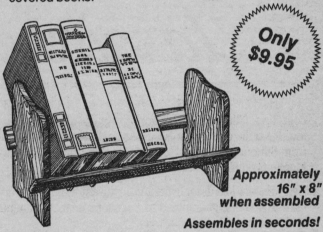

# COMING NEXT MONTH

**#616 TO MARRY AT CHRISTMAS—Kasey Michaels**
Elizabeth Chatham wasn't looking for romance . . . until she met dynamic Nicholas Lancaster and fell head over heels. Would wedding bells harmonize with sleigh bells?

**#617 AFTER THE STORM—Joan Smith**
Aspiring writer Susan Knight was more than curious about her mysterious new neighbor, Dan Ogilvy. She had to discover what the sexiest man she'd ever met was up to. . . .

**#618 IF DREAMS WERE WILD HORSES—Adeline McElfresh**
Ana-Maureen Salem thought she was fenced into her city life. But then she bought a wild horse and met Jeremy Rodriguez—the one man who could let her passion run free!

**#619 THE KERANDRAON LEGACY—Sara Grant**
The legacy of a magnificent Breton mansion stood between them, but one magical moonlit night Christie Beaumont lost her heart forever to devastating Luc Keraven. . . .

**#620 A MAN OF HER OWN—Brenda Trent**
Widow Kaye Wilson dreamed of building a life for herself and her daughter—without the help of a man. Then she met irresistible Whit Brooks. . . .

**#621 CACTUS ROSE—Stella Bagwell**
Years after he'd left her, rugged Tony Ramirez returned to help lovely Andrea Rawlins save her ranch. Could Andrea risk loving this masterful Texan again?

## AVAILABLE THIS MONTH:

# FOUR UNIQUE SERIES FOR EVERY WOMAN YOU ARE..

## *Silhouette Romance*

Love, at its most tender, provocative, emotional... in stories that will make you laugh and cry while bringing you the magic of falling in love.

*6 titles per month*

## *Silhouette Special Edition*

Sophisticated, substantial and packed with emotion, these powerful novels of life and love will capture your imagination and steal your heart.

*6 titles per month*

## *Silhouette Desire*

Open the door to romance and passion. Humorous, emotional, compelling—yet always a believable and sensuous story—Silhouette Desire never fails to deliver on the promise of love.

*6 titles per month*

## *Silhouette Intimate Moments*

Enter a world of excitement, of romance heightened by suspense, adventure and the passions every woman dreams of. Let us sweep you away.

*4 titles per month*

SILG-1R